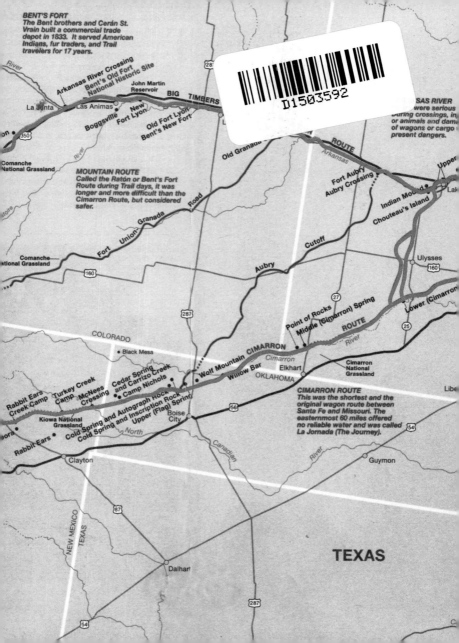

BENT'S FORT
The Bent brothers and Cerán St. Vrain built a commercial trade depot in 1833. It served American Indians, fur traders, and Trail travelers for 17 years.

Arkansas River Crossing
Bent's Old Fort National Historic Site

BIG TIMBERS

River

La Junta

Las Animas

Boggsville

John Martin Reservoir

New Fort Lyon

Old Fort Lyon

Bent's New Fort

350

Comanche National Grassland

Old Granada

MOUNTAIN ROUTE
Called the Ratón or Bent's Fort Route during Trail days, it was longer and more difficult than the Cimarron Route, but considered safer.

Fort Aubry
Aubry Crossing

Indian Mound

Chouteau's Island

...SAS RIVER
...were serious
During crossings, in...
or animals and dama...
of wagons or cargo...
present dangers.

ROUTE

Arkansas

Upper

Lak...

ational Grassland

Fort Union-Granada Road

160

287

Aubry

Cutoff

Ulysses

160

27

Point of Rocks
Middle (Cimarron) Spring

ROUTE

River

Lower (Cimarron

25

COLORADO

Black Mesa

Wolf Mountain **CIMARRON**

Willow Bar

Cimarron

Elkhart

Cimarron National Grassland

Rabbit Ears Creek Camp
Turkey Creek Camp
Cedar Spring and Carrizo Creek
McNees Crossing
Camp Nichols
Autograph Rock
Cold Spring and Inscription Rock
Cold Spring
Upper (Flag) Spring
Boise City

OKLAHOMA

Libe...

56

54

CIMARRON ROUTE
This was the shortest and the original wagon route between Santa Fe and Missouri. The easternmost 60 miles offered no reliable water and was called La Jornada (The Journey).

Kiowa National Grassland

...ora

Rabbit Ears

North

Canadian

River

Guymon

Clayton

87

NEW MEXICO
TEXAS

TEXAS

Dalhart

287

54

C...

Perilous Pursuit

on the Santa Fe Trail

Books by Inez Ross

The Strange Disappearance of Uncle Dudley:
A Child's Story of Los Alamos

The Bear and the Castle:
The James Oliver Curwood Story

The Adobe Castle:
A Southwest Gothic Romance

Persuaded:
A Great Lakes Story

Without A Wagon on the Santa Fe Trail

Perilous Pursuit on the Santa Fe Trail

Perilous Pursuit

on the Santa Fe Trail

Inez Ross

ASHLEY HOUSE

Perilous Pursuit
On the Santa Fe Trail

Library of Congress Control Number: 2005903933

Published by Ashley House
614 47th St.
Los Alamos NM 87544

ISBN: 9780966433753

ASHLEY HOUSE
www.ReadSouthwest.com

For Leland
my best buddy

Caveat

This is a work of fiction, but resemblance to some living persons is strictly intentional. Most of the Santa Fe Trail sites are real, but poetic license has produced some alterations: Kansas City has acquired a Westport Mansion, and the Eklund Hotel in Clayton, New Mexico, has acquired a ballroom with outside balcony.

Acknowledgments

I am indebted to many people for help in preparing this book. Lucille McCleskey listened to episodes and asked for more. Lynette Ross and Shermagne Gunn checked the story for plausibility and made suggestions, while Carolyn Robinson and Judith Janay read for style and clarity. Dexter Sutherland filled in the holes, and Phyllis Morgan edited for any remaining glitches.

D'Anne Andrykovich painted the cover scene, and book designer John Cole patiently packaged it all beautifully for the printer.

I thank the U.S. Park Service for the use of the Santa Fe Trail map and the Santa Fe Trail Association, especially the Corazon de los Caminos, and End of the Trail chapters, for the tours and talks that gave historical background for the book. The Los Alamos Writers Group did critiques and made suggestions.

Thanks also to Sir Arthur Conan Doyle for the loan of one of his villains.

Special Thanks

Thanks to the Hiking Ladies, the team who hiked with me from Santa Fe to Franklin and put up with their Trail Boss through the eight-year project. Our group adventure contributed to the ideas for this book. They are Judith Janay, Jennifer Reglien, Carolyn Robinson, and Phyllis Morgan.

I

The Train to Kansas City

"Wake up, Watling! We need to catch the train!"

I struggled upward out of a deep sleep, trying to remember where I was. I was dreaming I was crossing the prairie in a covered wagon. As I regained consciousness, I saw the framed picture of a Kansas wagon train on the far wall of the motel room and then realized I live in the twenty-first century, not the nineteenth.

This was the beginning of the most adventurous and unusual case I have yet recorded for my friend and employer Sheila Jones. As her amanuensis and assistant I have become increasingly involved in her exploits. And they have become increasingly more unusual and challenging as her expertise has attracted the notice of an ever widening circle of clients. Here we were in the town of Lawrence, Kansas, hundreds of miles from our Albuquerque base, supposedly on a vacation trip to a convention, but somebody had located us and was asking for help.

I looked at the clock on the bedside stand, then at the hotel window which revealed only darkness between the partially opened curtains. "It's only 4 a.m," I moaned. "Why so early?"

"The train to Kansas City leaves at 5:30 a.m. We need to meet a client in the sleeping car of that train."

Jones was already dressed in her tailored tan suit, which I knew meant business, and was brushing out the curls in her short gray hair.

I looked in the mirror at my own brown Clairol locks which stood in wild disarray above my puffy eyes. I grabbed the black dress I had worn for the concert the previous night and headed for the shower. Why did we have to go by train instead of by car? Why did we have to meet our client on the train instead of at the hotel? These were the puzzling questions I knew would be answered as we went.

In the shower I was still humming the tune "Perfidia" from the player-piano rendition I had heard the night before. Sherlock Holmes played the violin for his relaxation, but Sheila Jones' favorite leisure diversion was the player piano. The Keyboard Convention we had attended featured all kinds of piano demonstrations from concertos on a grand piano to folk songs on a concertina, but Jones preferred the player piano, especially the antique mechanical instrument which required pumping the pedals to force air through the perforated paper rolls. She enjoyed the athletic exercise, the music, and the fun of waving her hands over the keys as if depressing them herself.

Perfidia, I mused. It means *"Faithlessness."* Perhaps an omen of treachery or some other skulduggery to come. "Are we checking out for real, or are we coming back this evening? We'll need to come back here for the car, won't we?"

"We're checking out. The strange nature of this case may require spending some time in Kansas City, but we'll return on the train and pick up the car here." Jones was already in the hall and headed for the elevator as she spoke.

I hoped for time to grab a bagel in the hotel lobby and smear it with cream cheese, and I was dying for a cup of coffee, but the hotel had not yet put out the continental breakfast promised to guests.

"We'll get breakfast on the train, Watling. Hurry up." The stimulation of the upcoming adventure was enough for Jones, but I craved my wake-up caffeine.

The Southwest Chief Amtrak train was already at the station when we parked the car. Jones consulted the note in her pocket and said, "Car 330, Room 7," and led the way to the front of the train where she gave the name "Helen Stoner" (the name of our prospective client) to the car attendant. He took our bags and directed us up the inside stairway to the compartments on the upper level of the car.

Roomette Number 7 was a tiny space with seats intended for only two facing passengers. One seat was occupied by an attractive young woman with brown and blonde-streaked hair and a worried look.

"Oh, Mrs. Jones," she said. "I'm so glad you came. When I read in the paper about your solving the Swink Swindle case, I hoped that you could help me. I was worried you may not find me. I did not want to use my cell phone or try your hotel again. I'm nervous about this whole thing and such a scatterbrain I couldn't remember if I gave your housekeeper all the information and the right day. My sister always called me Bubblehead. I'm not really stupid, just terribly disorganized at times. Please sit down. I'm sorry there's not more room."

Though Jones is tall and thin, I am rather the opposite, so I offered to sit elsewhere in the coach section, but Sheila objected.

"We can squeeze in. There's plenty of room. I'm not 'Mrs,' just Sheila Jones. This is my assistant Dora Watling, who attends me in all my cases and to whom you may speak as if to me. Privacy is assured. We usually call each other by our last names and you're welcome to do the same." She motioned me to the seat next to her and closed the sliding glass door. She was about to draw the curtains to assure further privacy when the car attendant knocked and asked if we needed anything.

"Three coffees, black, please," Sheila ordered, and turned to Helen for confirmation.

"Oh, yes. That will be fine. How did you guess that I always drink coffee? I think I'm allergic to de-caf. Nothing could make me more nervous than I already am."

"I deduced by your jacket with logo that you're a student at the University here and on your way home to Kansas City for the Labor Day weekend. And college students usually acquire the coffee habit during long cramming hours for exams. But you must tell us the cause of your trouble and why you think we could help you."

"It's my stepfather, Dr. Sydney Roylott. I think he wants to kill me." She spoke very softly with a tremulous voice.

"Why do you think so?" Jones leaned forward to hear the details.

"My real father died when my sister Julia and I were five and eight years old. Julia is the older one. My mother remarried, but as she was always in frail health, she worried about the large inheritance left by my father. She set up a trust for us, and the terms specified that the money was to be controlled by my stepfather until we were twenty-one years old. She died three years later."

"And did your sister receive her inheritance? How old is she?"

"When she was twenty years old and a junior at Chicago Christian College she converted to Catholicism and joined the Sisterhood of St. Silencio. She went to live in an abbey which forbade all communication with the outside world. But just before her twenty-first birthday and before she went there, my stepfather tried to get her to sign away her inheritance to him. The Sisterhood forbids owning personal wealth, and he wanted it. She refused his request and instead, signed all her assets to the church. He became very angry. She is now twenty-three. I have not spoken to her for three years. Her name is changed and the only one knowing her address and allowed to communicate with her is my Aunt Lillian. I talk to Aunt Lillian, she lives in upper Michigan, whenever I can in order to find out how Julia is." There were tears in her eyes as she related this part of her story. She paused to look for her tissue box and was about to continue.

Here, the car attendant knocked on the door and presented a tray with coffee and muffins. He had auburn hair and fair skin, and his freckles gave him a youthful appearance. It was obvious that he had seen Helen Stoner before and was favorably impressed. "I added muffins to your order. They're especially good today," he said, smiling at her. He seemed ready to say more, but Jones thanked him summarily, took the tray, and closed the compartment door.

"So you're about to turn twenty-one and fear that your stepfather doesn't want to lose the other half of the trust? Has he asked you to sign any papers? Or has anything occurred to make you uneasy?" Jones took a cup of coffee, but refused the muffin as she watched Helen closely.

"Not yet. But my stepfather is a very strange man. Let me tell you what happened before Julia left for the abbey. Our house is huge and my stepfather has added an enormous library. One night when we were in the living room he asked Julia to get him a book from the top shelf of the library. She had to use the roller ladder and push it to the far side of the room. As she put her weight on the top step, it collapsed and she fell several feet to the hardwood floor. She hurt her head and broke her left arm in the fall. It wasn't till just before she left home that she told me she thought he had deliberately unscrewed the top step. We think he tried to kill her!"

"So her departure for the sisterhood was not just for her religion? She was perhaps fearful for her life?" asked Jones.

"Yes, and I know she is trying to warn me. Aunt Lillian said that her latest letter spoke of a "pickett pin," whatever that is, assuming I would understand. I have looked through the jewelry case my sister left me and can find no brooch looking like a pickett. I suppose she meant *pricking* pin, or something, and my mind goes to weird ideas like poison pins, hair pins, and such like."

7

"Tell me more about your stepfather," Jones said. "Are there other incidents that would indicate cruelty or greed?"

"He is very intelligent. His undergraduate degree is in fine arts from Yale and his doctorate is in American history from Michigan State University. He belongs to several organizations. I can't keep track of all his clubs, but I know he's out to meetings almost every night of the week. Sometimes he comes home very late and in a bad mood. He has a terrible temper and can't keep a butler for more than a year because of his crankiness and demanding personality. He loves all kinds of games and practical jokes. He has put us through some very scary situations with his treasure hunts. We enjoyed them at first, but they got more dangerous as we got older." She stopped to take another bite of her muffin and a sip of coffee.

Jones had put down her cup. She took out a yellow pad and commenced jotting notes on it. "Please explain these treasure hunts. What did they consist of?"

"Well, for instance, on Easter morning there would be a note on the table telling us to look in the refrigerator. In the refrigerator there would be maybe a candy egg and a note to look around the world. We knew that meant the big globe in the library. And under the globe would be another note telling us to look in the broom closet, and so forth. At the end we'd finally find the Easter basket of toys and candy."

8

"How, then, did it become dangerous?"

"Well, he'd send us outside, even across town or down to the river, and the directions got more and more tricky and hard to understand. One time we ended up at a fire station and had to phone him because no note was to be found. The shift at the station had changed, they'd swept the floor, and we were so embarrassed to be found looking under the firemen's beds. The police had been called and we were held for questioning until my stepfather arrived and explained everything.

"My birthday isn't till November 15. I am majoring in history and considering writing my thesis about the Santa Fe Trail, and because that is his main interest and area of expertise, he wants me to go on one of these big hunts down the entire Trail. He went to a convention or symposium recently, and I know he has been away laying out a route for me to follow. I'm afraid to go at his direction, but if I don't he'll be very angry. You see, he's a different person when he's angry. He becomes a madman. He smashes things. I've learned to get out and away when he gets into moods like that. You never saw such a change. It's as if he's a different person entirely or possessed by the devil."

Jones put her yellow pad into her briefcase, leaned back with her eyes closed for a few moments, then proposed our next steps in a plan. As we had an hour or so before reaching Kansas City, we would take breakfast in the dining car. Our conversation would reveal that we had only recently met and that Sheila Jones was a reporter and I a photographer for the Kansas City Star. We would be requesting an interview with Dr. Sydney Roylott of Westport Mansion to be used in a feature article regarding Great Men and Great Houses in the Kansas City area.

Helen Stoner believed that her stepfather would be flattered by that request and the subsequent attention from the press. She would tell him that she had met the reporter and photographer on the train and that they would be calling to request the interview.

We made our way to the dining car where we were seated at a table covered by a white cloth and decorated with fresh red carnations. "Not like the yellow roses of the old Super Chief days," remarked Jones. "But I know they have the same French toast we've always liked."

It was so. The French toast, the coffee, and the conversation all went down smoothly and our adventure was beginning to unfold with exciting prospects.

II

Escape from Westport Mansion

The Southwest Chief pulled into Kansas City just before 7:30 a.m. We detrained and were about to take the elevator up into Union Station, but Jones objected. "Remember the rule, Watling. If two floors or fewer, always take the stairs. One needs to take advantage of every exercise opportunity." It was no extra effort for Jones, who was a frequent jogger, and though I am more sedentary, I agreed, knowing the benefits of exercise. I recalled the case of the Bishop's Bathtub, which required Jones to run up seven flights of stairs and apprehend the criminal who had disconnected the elevator.

Helen laughed and complied also, and we climbed the stairs, then walked down a passageway which led into the great hall of the newly refurbished station. It had been renewed to its early 20th Century glory in the heyday of transcontinental trains and now boasted shops and restaurants along a hallway under the high vaulted ceiling. We said goodbye to Helen Stoner as she got into a taxi, and I was about to hail one for Jones and me when Jones again objected. "I think there's a Hyatt Hotel within walking distance. We can save some money and promote our health at the same time."

We checked into the hotel, and as it was yet too early to phone Dr. Roylott, laid out a plan for the morning. Jones wanted to find a library and absorb a little of the local history to learn something about Westport Mansion and possibly locate some information about Dr. Roylott himself. I was to find a photo shop and purchase a camera which would promote the impression that I was a press photographer.

We were successful on both counts, and when we met at the hotel again at noon, Jones was eager to reveal some interesting information. "The Westport section of this town is of great historic value. It was the original shipping depot, the place where the goods from the steamboats were loaded onto the wagons that were headed west. All three trails followed the same route out of town."

"What three trails?" I asked.

"The California, the Oregon, and the Santa Fe Trails. The stage station near Dr. Roylott's mansion was a final stopping place to graze the horses, get a good meal and adjust gear to continue west. The City and the Park Service have been trying to buy the mansion from Roylott and preserve it as part of the historic park, but he has refused to sell. He holds meetings of the Trail organizations there but wants to keep the house and land under his personal control.

"And what luck did you have finding a camera? That one looks too small to be a press camera."

"The clerk convinced me that the latest thing is a digital camera. It is more compact, and without the necessity of film, can transfer images directly to the press computers." I opened the box and displayed my purchase.

Jones seemed doubtful. "Let's hope that Roylott is also aware of the new technology and won't question your status. Read the directions and pack them away, so you'll appear to be familiar with the instrument. I'd like some photos, you realize, as part of this investigation."

Jones had placed a call to the Roylott Mansion and over lunch we experimented with the new camera while waiting for a return call. At one o'clock Roylott's butler called giving directions to the Mansion and saying we were invited to interview Dr. Roylott at four p.m.

I felt the need for a short nap, and was soon unconscious in our fourth floor room, but Jones stayed awake studying the camera, city maps, and a brochure of historical places. It seemed only minutes later that I heard, "Wake up, Watling! We're on our way."

A short taxi ride within the city brought us to a beautiful grove of huge trees with a large iron gate at the edge of the road. A straight gravel road led to a large white frame house, the original Westport Stage Station. Beyond it a curving road led through more dense foliage and ended at a palatial stone mansion, the home of Dr. Sydney Roylott.

The massive oaken door at the front looked forbidding, and as the road curved around to the side of the building, Jones directed the taxi driver to wait there in the porte cochere. Next to it was a hitching rail where a saddled horse stood panting as if having been recently exercised. As we got out of the taxi, a groom came up and led the horse away.

"I think Dr. Roylott must have just returned from a ride," observed Jones. "We may have to wait until he's ready to see us." And leaning toward me she privately added, "We may not be here long. While you were napping I called the newsroom at the Star, and although they approved the idea of an interview, they cautioned that it might be very difficult to obtain."

A butler met us at the side entrance and led us into a vestibule of dark wainscoted walls and fringed window hangings. We were led along a dark corridor lined with mounted animal trophy heads, portraits, and some glass aquarium-like cages. The dim light allowed no indication what kind of animals most of them held, but as we passed near the end of the hall I saw a huge snake in the container nearest the door. Then we entered the big library where Dr. Roylott himself stood in riding boots and leather jacket, a tall man of massive build, gray hair and mustache. His florid face showed the result of recent exertion and caused his bushy black eyebrows to contrast all the more with his gray hair. He held a riding whip and was tapping it impatiently against his right boot.

"Sorry to keep you waiting," he began. "My daughter told me that two reporters were interested in the Santa Fe Trail and would like to see my collection of books and manuscripts."

"Thank you very much for taking the time to talk to us. I am Sheila Jones and this is photographer Dora Watling."

I snapped a photo of him and turned the camera dial to "movie mode."

Roylott frowned and said, " You may take photos of anything in my collection, but no personal photos, please, of me or the house. The press already has plenty of pictures. If you are Trail buffs, you are welcome here, but I ask you to put away the camera."

I apologized and brought the camera down, but before I closed the shutter, I captured the view of the far wall with the tall wheeled ladder against the shelves of books.

He led us across the room to a long glass-covered case containing a huge map of the midwestern states. Across the middle, was shown the Santa Fe Trail, beginning in Missouri, extending all across Kansas, and going into Colorado before turning south into New Mexico. One branch of the Trail went more southwesterly across the western end of Oklahoma and joined the other part north of Santa Fe.

"I thought the Trail began at Kansas City," I remarked innocently.

Dr. Roylott positively scowled and, using his whip handle as a pointer, explained the extent of the Trail. "You are not a Trail person, I see. Your companion knows, I'm sure that although this map shows the branching of the California and Oregon Trails near Kansas City, you need to realize that the Santa Fe Trail was the first western trail. It was not primarily a road of settlement or exploration, but a commercial venture, having traders going from Mexico to Missouri, as well as American entrepreneurs headed from here to Santa Fe. Although animals, Indians, and earlier explorers probably traveled the area first, it was William Becknell of Franklin, Missouri, who began trading with Santa Fe in 1821 and is credited with establishing it as a commercial route. He is the Father of the Santa Fe Trail."

"I've never heard of Franklin," I said. My comment brought a frown to Jones' face at that comment, and I began to realize my comments may jeopardize the interview. A good press photographer leaves the questions to the interviewer. Was Roylott beginning to see we were frauds? He was warming to his subject, however, and took a professorial pleasure in informing us.

"The goods came by steamboat up the Missouri River and were loaded into wagons at Franklin. In later years the shipping point moved to Independence, and later to Westport, which is as you know, a part of Kansas City now."

I ventured one more question. "Is there still a trail you can walk along, like the Appalachian Trail?"

"Oh, no. Much of the Trail has disappeared," he replied. "When the railroad reached Santa Fe in 1880, there was no longer a need for a wagon road. The homesteaders and farmers plowed the land and in only a few places can you see the traces of the Trail where the wagon wheels left deep ruts. But the highways that go southwest in the general vicinity have been labeled as the Auto Tour Route of the Santa Fe Trail. It was designated a National Historic Trail in 1978. Signs along the highways that parallel the Trail designate it as the 'Auto Tour Route' with a covered wagon logo."

"Can you show us more of your collection?" Jones asked. "I am interested in this wooden gadget and the little moon-shaped pieces of metal."

"The wooden affair with the pump-like handle is a wagon jack, used to prop up a wagon when repairing a wheel. The little crescent-shaped pieces of metal are actually oxen shoes. Oxen were preferred over mules by some traders because, although slower, they were less subject to stealing by the Indians."

Maybe Roylott saw the little indicator light on my camera, showing it was still operating. He suddenly turned from the case and said, "Could you show me your press pass, please?"

Jones replied, "We don't have our cards with us, but the city editor is expecting a feature. You can call him for confirmation."Jones realized that Roylott's tone of voice and the tap-tap-tap of the whip handle were indications that the interview was over.

Suddenly Roylott blurted out, "I think you are here under auspices other than that of the newspaper. I am not to be made a fool of by prying women!"

"I'm sorry that we have earned your distrust," replied Jones. "We have intruded on your time. We appreciate your admitting us to your beautiful home and giving us interesting information. Thank you and goodbye."

As we headed toward the door, Roylott called out, "Give me the camera! Unless I see that those photos are erased, I am calling the law!"

But we were already descending the steps and hurrying into the waiting taxi. I was glad to escape and feared that Jones would blame me for "blowing our cover," but as we climbed back into the cab, Jones seemed pleased with the encounter. "Good job, Watling! Your camera with no flash was a provident choice. I saw that you took a few unobserved shots. And while you were asking questions I observed the room and the ladder with its missing top step. There was a small throw rug, the only one in the room, covering an area in the corner where Julia Stoner may have fallen. It all corroborates Helen Stoner's story and leads me to believe we may be right in accepting her suspicions. I believe we have ourselves a case indeed."

As the cab rounded the curve in front of the white frame house, we could see Helen Stoner running out from the porch there and waving at us to stop. She was out of breath, and as Jones opened the door to speak to her, she thrust a piece of paper at us and said, "Franklin, Missouri. Meet me at the Mansion. Please go tomorrow." Jones was about to ask for further information, but she closed the door, waved us onward, and pointed to the road behind us.

Dr. Roylott was mounted on his horse and galloping toward us at a furious pace. Helen ran back to the stage-station porch, and Dr. Roylott, realizing that a horseback chase was no match for a taxi, gave up the chase as we drove out onto the main road. The big gate clanged shut behind us.

III

A Singular Spirit in the Celtic Pub

We were relieved at our escape, but wondered if Roylott had seen Helen speaking to us. "I hope he doesn't use that whip on any human," I said. "I'm worried about Helen's safety."

"She knows our hotel and will call us if there's a problem," Jones replied. "But now we need to find this Mansion. All it says here is *The Mansion*. That must be the name of the hotel. We'll catch the train tonight back to Lawrence and get the car. The Missouri map will show us where Franklin is."

"That's the place where the Santa Fe Trail began, according to Roylott," I said.

The Southwest Chief was not due till after 10 p.m. and Jones decided we should add to our knowledge of

Trail history by dining in the Westport area. The Celtic Pub was listed in the phone directory as The Oldest Pub in the Oldest Building in Kansas City, so there we betook ourselves for a supper of corned beef and cabbage with a draft of Santa Fe Cider.

The establishment was dimly lighted with dark oaken walls and high beamed ceiling. A balcony with tables ran around three sides of the restaurant area, but seemed empty of diners. At the back of the room a small fireplace gave a cheery glow reflected on the faces of two men sitting near it. We had finished eating and were having a cup of coffee when the two men from the fireplace asked to join our table. We had exchanged the usual pleasantries about where each is from, and so forth, when Jones abruptly asked, "Have you ever heard of the man Roylott who lives near here?"

The first man, a chubby-cheeked talker with goatee and raspy voice, replied, "Bloke that lives in the big stone house behind the stage-station park? Oh yeah, he's some big cheese. Runs lots of clubs and businesses around here. Used to come here for a pint now and then, but got mad at the bartender one time and doesn't come 'round any more."

The other man, a slim dark-haired man with wire-rim glasses, added, "You don't want to get him mad, though. He's the strongest feller I've ever seen. See that fireplace poker over there that's bent nearly double? It was a straight iron poker that he picked up and twisted over to show his strength. He dared anyone to straighten it back if they could. No one could and it sits there like that to this day."

Jones and I exchanged knowing glances and turned to hear the music. Near the bar a combo of accordion, fiddle, and drum was plinking out frontier songs, and some delighted listeners joined in singing along.

Buffalo gals, won't you come out tonight
And dance by the light of the moon.

Then Irish tunes were requested and two men near the bar began singing.

Did you ever look into an Irishman's shanty
Where money is scarce and whisky is plenty?
A three-legged stool and a table to match
An egg in the corner all ready to hatch.

An elderly lady stood up and started to jig. A younger woman at her table, probably her daughter, tried to pull her back to her chair, but the singing men called out, "Let her dance! Go Granny!" And she continued with sprightly hops and kicks to the amusement and clapping of the entire room.

As the laughter subsided I thought I heard a chuckle from the balcony above, but because that area was unlighted in contrast to the lamps and candles around us, I could not detect the source of the laughter. The musicians announced a short break and one heavy bald man called out, "Who'll pump?" and pointed to an old upright piano in the far corner. Jones realized that here was her chance to examine an antique player piano and stood up quickly with an "I will." She was eager to see what music rolls were in the piano bench and in the case on top. The sing-along crowd gathered around and she began pumping to "When Irish Eyes are Smiling," followed by "I'll be in Scotland Afore Ye".

I don't know what caused me to look up at the balcony again, but this time I saw there a lone figure, all in black. A woman wearing a bonnet was shaking her head slowly as if disapproving of the noise below. Then she looked at me and pointed her finger at me. I pointed at myself as if to ask "Me?" and she nodded, then pointed down at her table top. I was the only one facing away from the piano, but still thinking there must be a mistake, I decided to respond to her invitation.

The stairway was in a back corner, and I hesitated before climbing it. It looked rather steep and narrow, almost a ladder, and in the dim light I couldn't attest to its stability. But up I went and to my surprise found no one at any of the tables there! Thinking she must have gone out another way, I continued around the balcony, but there seemed to be no other exit than the stairway by which I'd ascended. I saw a paper napkin with some words printed on it at the table where I'd seen the figure. I took it and climbed back down the creaky stairway.

Rather shaken by the experience, I sat down again and in the light of the candle at our table read, "BEWAR THE PICKE." Jones continued pumping, the piano continued plinking the rinky-tink tunes, and the crowd around the piano continued singing along, all unaware that I had seen what must have been a ghost. The only person seemingly oblivious to the musical party was the bartender, a thin man with wispy brown hair and a natty bow tie. I approached him and asked, "Did you see a woman seated in the balcony tonight?"

He stopped polishing the beer glass in his hand, put down the towel and smiled at me. "Begorra! Lucille is back," he said. "What did she say to ye?"

"Nothing," I replied. "But she motioned me to come up there, and all I found was this paper napkin on the table."

He looked at it and shook his head slowly. "I dinna know what it means, but I think you'll be getting a warnin' aboot something. You see, she's a beautiful Scottish lady who died many years ago. This pub stands on the site where her house was. She sometimes appears when a Scottish tune is played, but aren't you the lucky one, now. No one has seen her for aye these many years."

The piano music stopped and Jones returned to our table. When I told her about my spectral experience, she began to laugh. "Watling, you're seeing things! Our cider was supposed to be non-alcoholic. I'm wondering if yours was a wee bit spiked? You did go back for a second glass, I noticed. Someone left that napkin up there and the bartender took advantage of you to have a little fun. The trio is beginning to play again, and maybe we'd better leave before they play any more Scottish tunes."

Still visibly shaken, I agreed it was time to go. I put the napkin into my pocket, resolving to read it again in the daylight, when I was calmer, and followed Jones to our hotel.

We climbed aboard the Chief again, this time in coach class, but because the seat could be tilted far back, I soon lost consciousness as the gentle rocking vibration of the train took us westward.

It seemed as if no time at all had elapsed when I heard the conductor coming through the train calling, "Lawrence! Lawrence next!" I saw that Jones had been studying the map and as she folded it up, she said, " We'll drive east into Missouri tomorrow and find the beginning of the Santa Fe Trail and the Mansion Helen referred to."

IV

Franklin, The Trail Begins

North of the Interstate highway on the map was listed
the small town of Boonville, and nearby a tiny dot was
labeled New Franklin. It was lunch time, and as we
exited the freeway and drove into Boonville, Jones
suggested, "This corner cafe looks like a good place to
eat and get further directions."

As we parked the car I said, "We must be near our
goal. Look at the side of the building." The entire side
of the two-story restaurant was decorated with a huge
mural depicting covered wagons, Indians and fron-
tiersmen, and at the base was painted a sidewheeler
steamboat bringing goods up the Missouri River.

As we finished our cherry pie after a delicious lunch,
the waitress called our attention to a comely gray-haired

lady at a nearby table. "If you're interested in Franklin and the Santa Fe Trail, talk to Mrs. Opal here. She's our history expert."

We walked over and introduced ourselves, asking about the route to Franklin. "Are you looking for New Franklin," she asked, "or just Franklin, the original place where the Santa Fe Trail began?" She spoke with ingratiating eagerness and I detected a twinkle in her eye as if she were about to let us in on a surprise.

After we confirmed it was the latter, she offered to lead us there. "I'm ready to leave, and if you'll follow my car, we'll be there in ten minutes."

Following her car, through the streets of Boonville and up a steep hill, brought us to a park overlooking the Missouri River. We parked and looked down from the high hill at the tree-lined river below us. Beyond the opposite bank flat open fields edged with green trees stretched into the distance, with no sign of a town.

"There you are," she said. "That's the site of the original Franklin. The town was washed away when the river flooded in 1829. But some folks settled a few miles away on higher ground. That's where the town of New Franklin is today."

Jones was peering through her binoculars. "I see some sort of fence and flagpole over there," she said. "Is there a historical marker of some sort?"

"Oh, yes. The Historical Society has put up information boards and markers. There is also a monument telling of the first newspaper, the one Becknell advertised in when he was looking for men to go on the first trading expedition. He's considered the Father of the Santa Fe Trail, you know."

"Is there a hotel called The Mansion in New Franklin?" asked Jones.

"You must be referring to Rivercene, the big house that's a bed-and-breakfast inn. It's just over the bridge, before you come to New Franklin. But if you have time, come on up into New Franklin. That's where most of the Trail travelers end their treks. The bicycle group that rides the Trail every other year ends up there. And the Historical Society always welcomes Trail travelers at the Senior Center and the Museum on the main street. There's a big monument and message boards there, too."

We thanked her and promising to visit the New Franklin Museum, headed back down the hill to cross the river on the big bridge near the restaurant. There was the Rivercene, a huge three-story mansion with a mansard roof and a side tower. Tall trees lined the parking area and a curving balustrade welcomed visitors to a double door on the balconied porch. We rang and were met by hostess Merijo Merton, a square-built, elegant dowager who welcomed us cordially and declared we had been expected.

"Helen Stoner reserved rooms for you. She plans to arrive this evening also," she said. We stepped from the foyer into a huge sitting room which was decorated in a style reminiscent of southern plantations. There was a grand piano and near the fireplace life-size standing cutouts of Scarlett O'Hara and Rhett Butler faced each other as if they had just stepped out of the film *Gone with the Wind*.

We were given a tour of the house which was built in 1869 by Captain Kinney, who had made his fortune as a riverboat trader and later founded the Kinney Shoes Corporation. Flooding of the Missouri River had once inundated the first floor of the mansion, but the Mertons were refurbishing the entire building to restore it to its former glory.

Mrs. Merton led us up a grand staircase while she explained the history and renovations. "Our third story is still cluttered with lumber and tools, but we do have a single room for one of you at the top of the third floor stairway which has just been completed. The gold and ecru set off the velvet coverings nicely. I think you'll be very comfortable."

I volunteered to take the upper room, while Jones and Helen would have the tiny pink nursery room on the first floor. The two flights of stairs would contribute to my exercise requirement, I reasoned. Mr. Bill Merton, a dignified gentleman in a red plaid weskit, came out of the kitchen bearing a tray of tiny sandwiches. "Time for tea, Ladies," he announced. "Here is the Rivercene specialty. It comes with sparkling cranberry juice." The teapot was still brewing, and the aroma coming from the kitchen promised some kind of ginger cake or pastry to follow.

We were concerned as the hour grew late and Helen had not arrived, but the Mertons kept us entertained with riverboat tales and dismissed our fears with the theory that Helen had planned to arrive via the slower river roads. "She said she's doing research on the Trail and probably wanted to drive by way of Fort Osage," Mr. Merton explained. "While we're waiting we can entertain ourselves with the Becknell Skit. If the Wallends arrive, we'll have enough people for all the parts. Guests always like it."

"I hope this weather doesn't make the river road dangerous," I commented. "It seems to have started raining in earnest." Their responses were interrupted by the ringing of the bell and the expected Wallend couple arrived. Lois, a perky blonde, and Jim, her tall gray-haired husband, were a retired couple on their way to Florida. They always made the Rivercene their Missouri stop, were on a friendly basis with the hosts, and immediately asked if there would be the usual skit.

"And where is Giselle?" Jim asked. As if on cue, a huge black French poodle came bounding from the kitchen to be welcomed by the Wallends, scolded by the Mertons, and told to sit by the fireplace till after tea. The tea table conversation was an exchange of news concerning the travel destinations of the guests, the state of the weather, and finally, the arrangements for re-enacting the Santa Fe Trail Skit.

After considerable shuffling and assigning of roles, it was decided that Jim Wallend would play the part of Becknell, Bill Merton would be P.O.P. (Public Opinion Personified) and Lois Wallend, having played the part before, would read the introduction as Narrator. A fire was built in the big living room fireplace, and chairs were being arranged when the bell rang again and Helen Stoner was admitted, rather wet and windblown, but relieved to find us there. We reciprocated the sentiment and were further relieved to hear that Roylott remained ignorant regarding our association with Helen.

"He thinks you were from the Park Commission trying to insinuate yourselves into his good graces for purchase of the Westport Mansion property. I'm so glad you're here. I was delayed in packing and didn't come by the river roads, but I'm looking forward to having you with me to explore the Trail. Mrs. Merton helped Helen with her coat and remembered, "There was a phone message for you from your stepfather. He said your first stop should be the flagpole and monument at the site of Old Franklin. I hope the weather will clear for you."

As if in comment on her last remark, a peal of thunder rumbled overhead, and the lights in the room flickered. But after the initial surprise, we settled into the belief that the storm was passing. Helen was shown to her room, then given some hot tea and a place by the fire, and the play began. (I was later given a copy of the script, a part of which I reproduce here.)

Narrator

Imagine yourself, my Friends, to be living here in 1821. The edge of Missouri is the edge of the American Frontier. Far to the west is the Spanish colony of Mexico and between is the wilderness of Indian Territory, largely unexplored. We see William Becknell seated in his living room looking dejectedly into the fire and thinking of his bleak prospects, as he imagines a conversation with Public Opinion Personified.

P.O.P.

Well, you're in a fine pickle now! Bankrupt and almost in jail for debt.

Becknell

Sure glad I at least had a friend to bail me out.

P.O.P.

But what now? This recession doesn't leave you with many resources.

Becknell

Except another venture. I have goods enough for a trading expedition to New Spain.

P.O.P.

What! And risk being thrown into jail there? Spain doesn't allow traders from the States. You heard what happened to Zeb Pike and those other fellows who went down exploring.

Becknell

I've heard that Mexico is about to declare independence from Spain. Their old laws may be done away with.

P.O.P.

But even if they don't put you in jail, what makes you think they'll buy your goods?

Becknell

All the manufactured goods the Mexicans get now have traveled two thousand miles up from Vera Cruz port after coming from Spain. The market is

ripe for selling cloth, tools, and good kitchen ware
from our country. I know I could make a profit.

Before Public Opinion Personified could reply, the play was interrupted by Giselle who jumped up from her spot near the fire and ran to the foyer, where she began barking at the door. We could see the bottom of the grand starcase from our seats in the living room and watched in interest as Giselle uttered low growls and cowered back as if watching someone approach the staircase, then gaze upward still growling, as if an invisible guest were climbing the stairs. Bill Merton put down his play script, and spoke to Giselle, then went to the door, checked the porch, re-locked the door, and turning on the foyer lights went up the staircase. He returned with the comment, "She's probably just nervous with this storm. Calm down, Giselle. You're O.K. Let's get on with our play."

There was an uneasy stir in the company, but Bill picked up his script and resumed reading.

P.O.P.

That ad you put in the paper asking for 70 men to
join you on an expedition to "Trade with the
Indians" isn't fooling anyone. Everyone knows
your real goal is Santa Fe. And only five men have
signed up to join you. Are you crazy?

And before poor Becknell could reply, another clap of thunder echoed overhead and the lights flickered again, then dimmed, and went out completely, leaving us in the dark. We chuckled as Lois announced, "Ladies and Gentlemen! Be calm. Remain seated. We will resume the show shortly. Remain for Act II to find out if William Becknell really is crazy, if he really did go to Santa Fe, if he got arrested for bringing foreign goods, or if he died of thirst in the desert."

However, the scramble for flashlights and lanterns, plus the lateness of the hour, resulted in postponement of the play with the cheerful announcement from Merijo Merton that we all had rainchecks for the rest of the play the next night.

I did not admit my nervousness about being the only guest on the third floor, but Jones had a good deal of fun at my expense. "Well, Watling, you'll be keeping company with a ghost, I guess. Maybe it's the same one you saw in Westport."

Helen added, "These old houses could be haunted. Mrs. Merton, have you had spirit visits before?" Merijo denied ever having had unusual visitations, and Bill commented, "Well now that Giselle has seen one, we can advertise this as a Haunted Mansion and bookings will really increase!"

Taking my flashlight, I climbed the stairs with an air of bravado, but I was remembering my experience with the Lucille apparition in Westport. Was it possible for a ghost to follow someone into another state? Was I doomed to be pursued by a spirit while trying to help with the investigation of a crazy Trail aficionado? I was too tired to be afraid of the shadows in my elegant boudoir, and I fell asleep almost immediately under the cloud-soft duvet.

But I was wakened twice in the night by the sound of footsteps which seemed to be coming from above me. From an attic? The roof? Each time the sounds seemed to increase and then fade as if someone wearing heavy shoes were pacing back and forth. As the sound of the steps faded, I turned and slept again, only to be re-awakened when they grew louder. I rationalized that late guests had arrived and were being housed in the unfinished rooms near me, or that workmen had arrived early and were preparing to resume working on the renovations.

But in the morning I did not see any new guests, nor did I inquire about the coming of any workmen, and I dismisssed Jones' comment about my rather haggard looks with the excuse that I never sleep well in a strange bed that's too soft.

The sun was shining, power had been restored, and the Mertons served a delicious breakfast, over which we discussed our plans. Helen was eager to see the Old Franklin site, and Jones and I were wondering what message from Roylott, if any, would be there, or if he would appear in person. We gave our regrets that we'd be missing the conclusion of the Becknell skit, said goodbye to our hosts and the Wallends, and headed for Old Franklin site.

V

Crossing the Big Muddy

At Old Franklin site the nicely tended green area with markers and a flag pole kept our attention as we browsed the posted historical information. Jones and I had parked a little distance away near two cars belonging to other tourists. We did not want to be seen by Roylott in case he was waiting nearby. When we saw no indication of his presence, we strolled the area with Helen keeping a wary eye out for any approaching cars. Helen was excited to be beginning her Trail trek and began taking notes.

"Isn't this amazing? To think there was a town here, complete with newspaper offices and businesses on the edge of the frontier! Now there should be some kind of message from my stepfather."

We helped her search the entire monument area for some time with no results, until Jones suddenly said, "Aha, Watling. Here we have it!" And she produced a tiny green vial with a cork stopper and a rolled paper inside. Handing it to Helen, she explained, " I knew Roylott would have protected any message from the elements and concealed it from the eyes of casual observers, so I examined the rounded end of that railing which I found had been hollowed out and the little container inserted with the cork flush with the end to appear as part of the wood."

She helped extract the cork and Helen read the enclosed message.

You will get the information in the lunchroom of the Huston Tavern in Arrow Rock, across the Missouri River.

Jones and I were ready to follow her by car across the bridge at Boonville and head for the town of Arrow Rock, but Helen said, "Wait! There's no rush, and I have an idea. I learned in my research that Becknell crossed the river near here to get to Arrow Rock. There used to be a ferry in olden times. Wouldn't it be fun to cross the river in a boat? Someone around here must rent rowboats and could take us to the other side. I'd like to follow Becknell's original route as close as possible."

"Mrs. Opal said we should see the museum at New Franklin before we leave, anyway," I said. "Maybe we could find out there where the actual ferry crossing was and whether there's a place to row across."

At the New Franklin Museum we met Joyce Miesbyer, a comely lady with startling blue eyes. As president of the Historical Society, she gave us a cordial welcome and showed us around the building which housed a wealth of interesting objects and documents. She didn't give us much hope of locating Becknell's original river crossing, but said, "Yes, I can get you a boat. The river has changed a lot since 1821, and we'll have to go a little upstream to cross, and then land a little downstream from Arrow Rock, but you'll be duplicating his route as near as possible for modern times."

Her phone call to the boat owner was followed by a discussion of the logistics of shuttling the cars, so we'd end up with transportation in Arrow Rock. She drove her car, and we followed in Jones' car with Helen behind us, south along the Missouri River. We ended several miles away from Franklin and stopped at a tributary of the Missouri called the Lamine. Leaving Helen's car there, we drove back up the Missouri to quite a distance above Franklin where we were amazed to find a thirty-four foot pontoon boat anchored in a cove with a gangplank ready for our boarding.

A muscular young man wearing a captain's cap, white t-shirt and canvas pants was introduced as Admiral

Nelson. Seeing our surprise at finding such a large boat, he explained, "The river is too full and too fast to be crossing in a rowboat. And there are cliffs directly across, with no anchorage area, so you'll get across the river, but with a longer ride downstream. Here are deck chairs, or you can sit on the sofa. I have cold drinks in the cooler for us."

So we relaxed and enjoyed an hour's ride along the Big Muddy Missouri, watching silver carp leap from the water, some even striking the sides of the boat. The tree-lined shore gave very few breaks for views of any habitation, and our comments reflected our amazement at the contrast between nineteenth-century river crossings and our own party-boat trip. The Admiral and Joyce entertained us by singing seafaring ditties:

Over the sea, let's go men!
We're shoving right off, we're shoving right off
   again
Nobody knows where or when
We're shoving right off, we're shoving right off
   again
It may be Shanghai, farewell and goodbye
Sally and Sue, don't be blue
We'll just be gone for years and years and then
We're shoving right off for home again!

We disembarked near a bridge on the Lamine River

where the Admiral had a truck and boat trailer for loading his craft, and after riding back in Helen's car to retrieve the other car and cross the river again on the modern bridge at Boonville, we found the afternoon well advanced. We said our thanks and goodbyes with a sense of great accomplishment at finishing the first leg of the Santa Fe Trail in such an unexpected way.

VI

Peril at Arrow Rock

As we drove into the town of Arrow Rock, Helen exclaimed, "This looks like a historical Disney Land!" The little frame houses, log cabins, and green lawns along the narrow streets certainly gave the impression of a quaint tourist village. But a closer look at the gabeled structures and at the carefully carved limestone gutters, laid down by slave labor many years ago, gave the picture of the real frontier. We learned that Arrow Rock was a National Historic Landmark as well as a State Historic Site.

We walked along the canopied boardwalk and found the two-story brick building with the wooden sign Huston Tavern hanging from a gibbet pole in front. A big white cat was trying unsuccessfully to sneak in as the door opened. Inside there were several dining rooms and a store offering items that would have been for sale in frontier days. We browsed the supply store then went into the first dining room for lunch. Helen inquired if there had been any messages left for her.

"Helen Stoner? No, I don't recall seeing any messages, but I'll ask in the office," our waitress replied. "Have you taken the walking tour yet?"

We explained that we had only just arrived and then asked what the main attractions were. " You must visit the Sappington house. Dr. Sappington was the man who first promoted quinine pills for the treatment of malaria. He sold the pills along the Trail and saved many lives."

"Isn't there a famous artist also associated with this village?" asked Helen.

"Oh, yes. See that picture over there of the man dancing? That's the famous *Jolly Boatmen* painting by George Caleb Bingham. His house has been restored and furnished as it was when he lived here. You should see that too."

"Do you really have buffalo and elk burgers on the lunch menu? I'd like to have a buffalo burger."

She acquiesced, and Jones and I followed suit with the same order. We sat near the fireplace which displayed busts of Lewis and Clark on the mantel. Helen and I faced the doorway where we could see other tourists entering, but Jones was facing the window near our table and seemed interested in the wavy panes of leaded glass.

Just as the waitress returned bearing a huge tray of food and drinks, Jones backed away from the table. At the same time the cat, let in by an entering customer, ran toward the kitchen. The waitress, backing away from Jones, stumbled over the cat and her tray went flying. A waiter dived unsuccessfully for the cat, shouting, "Fluffy!" The resulting three-way crash between Jones, our waitress and the waiter completed the debacle, which resulted in flying plates and cutlery, and buffalo burgers sliding across the floor. We jumped up to avoid the water pooling on our table. But the strangest thing was that Jones stood suddenly and ran toward the entrance, calling back a quick apology. The cat had escaped the clutches of the stumbling waiter and was now headed out the door also with a burger patty in its mouth.

After the laughter, the apologies, and the cleanup, the waitress came with the news that there were no more buffalo burgers, but said she could bring us elk burgers instead. We accepted that offer and our order was entered. As we waited to be served, we wondered what had caused Jones' sudden exit and why she had not returned. I did not think she had become ill suddenly, so I surmised that she must have seen something through the window that caused her rapid exit. I was proved correct after a few minutes.

"I saw a woman fall trying to cross the road," Jones explained. "She was having a hard time trying to get up. Her son ran up just as I got to her, and she's O.K., but I thought she was alone and needed help." She continued eating her burger in silence and her demeanor suggested there may be part of her story left untold.

After lunch, my suspicion deepened when she said, "You two can go on to the Bingham house. I'm going to report that loose brick where she fell. I'll meet you at Dr. Sappington's, or if I'm delayed, I'll see you in the museum."

She was delayed. We had inquired again without success for a message from Roylott, completed the tour of both houses, browsed all the displays in the entire museum, and were watching the film about the history of Arrow Rock in the Museum Theater before she returned. We were lingering after the show to admire the map diagram of the Santa Fe Trail that stretched the entire length of both walls in the museum. Jones waited until the other tourists had left the theater and then said quietly, " I don't think you'll find any messages from Dr. Roylott. If my observations are correct, your stepfather tried to poison you in the Huston Tavern."

VII

Sad News at Marshall

We were stunned. "How? Poison? How do you know?" Our questions tumbled out as we sat down to listen to Jones' explanation.

"I ran from the dining room when I saw Roylott leaving the back door of the restaurant and crossing the green area to the next street. He disappeared beyond a line of cars parked near a wooded area, so I turned back, figuring he must have just left the expected message.

"As I approached the back of the restaurant, I saw the chef and a waiter standing over the cat which was retching and writhing on the ground. The men stood by, watching helplessly. The chef looked up as I approached and said, 'Choked on the piece of meat she grabbed.' But in a whispered aside to the waiter, he said, 'Cancel all buffalo orders.'

"I asked if I could take the cat to a veterinarian, and after they decided Fluffy really was seriously ill, the chef said, 'The animal hospital is in the town of Marshall, west of here.' The waiter brought a little rag rug from the tavern and while we wrapped the cat in it, I asked if any strangers had recently visited the kitchen. They replied in the negative but said the food inspector had just been there.

"Their description of the inspector tallied exactly with that of Dr. Roylott. 'Big tall man with heavy black eyebrows.' They said he did show the proper Inspector identification, but paid attention to the meat only, and seemed in rather a hurry.

"The drive over to Marshall and back caused my delay in joining you here. We'll leave Fluffy there overnight and hope it wasn't food poisoning that made her sick. I suggest we get a motel there for tonight."

Helen was trembling and with tear-filled eyes said, "It must be true. He is a terrible man. And I was so hoping I was wrong in my suspicions. I have put all of us in danger. What will he try next?"

"I think he intended the game to end here," replied Jones. "So it's unlikely he left any directions to the next Trail site for you. Do you plan to continue the trip?"

"The next major stop is Fort Osage. I wanted to get photos there too. What should I do?"

"Do you think he's headed back to Westport? My suggestion is for you to call him there, as if everything is fine, except that you could find no message in Arrow Rock. You have no definitive proof of his evil intent, and he must not suspect that you do, or that we are watching him. We'll continue down the Trail with you and try to anticipate his next move."

"Do you still want to come with me?" Helen asked. "I am putting all of us in danger by continuing this crazy game."

At this point the docent came to close the theater doors, and our conversation came to a stop, but Jones' nod and resolute expression showed a determination to pursue her plan.

Our motel in Marshall was Marshall Station, designed to look like an old-style railroad depot, complete with an antique baggage cart on the platform near the entrance. Helen and I were finishing breakfast in the lobby the next morning and looking at all the railroad memorabilia near the fireplace. Jones had risen and departed at dawn, leaving a note that she'd gone to the pet hospital and would call as soon as she found out about Fluffy's condition. I was examining a shelf of train books when the desk clerk, a young man in engineer overalls and spiked hair, came over to me and said, "Room thirteen? There's a call for you. You can take it here at the desk if you wish."

It was Jones. She reported that the cat had died and she would continue waiting there for an autopsy or cause-of-death report. She told us to visit the museum or take a city tour and we'd meet at the motel around noon.

"Poor Fluffy!" cried Helen. "She probably saved our lives by tripping the waitress and spilling that tray. How could my stepfather have poisoned those burgers?"

"Let's wait and see," I replied. "It may be a wrong assumption on our part. How did Roylott sound when you spoke with him on the phone last night?"

"He seemed rather annoyed and quite brusque, rather than surprised. He said he'd left word at the Tavern for me to continue to Fort Osage. He also made some crude comments about the stupidity of Arrow Rock Park people in general."

Jones commented, "I suppose it would be difficult to tell if his anger resulted from his poisoning plan gone awry, or from the annoyance that a message was not delivered."

The desk clerk approached and, probably having heard a part of our conversation said, "We don't have a regular tour of the town, but I can direct you to a memorial of a famous pet. Have you heard of Jim the Dog?"

When we replied in the negative, he seemed pleased to tell us how to reach the memorial in downtown Marshall. "It's in Ripley's Believe It or Not, too!" he added.

Following his sketched map, we drove downtown and found an entire lot between the commercial buildings dedicated to a garden with statue, fountain, and sign-boards telling the story of Jim the Dog, the psychic canine who seemed to understand human speech and could predict the future. His owner could instruct him to 'Find the lady carrying a red purse,' or 'Go to the stable door of the horse who will win tomorrow's race,' and Jim the Dog would invariably be correct! His owner was once told to leave the hotel where they were staying because of a warning from race officials regarding threats for the dog's safety.

"Fakery," said Jones when we told her about it later. "The dog was smart enough to read secret signals from his owner, and the owner was probably in cahoots with the underworld of race fixing. It's fortunate that Fluffy the Cat was not as smart as Jim the Dog. The pet hospital report was that Fluffy had indeed eaten poisoned meat. Lucky for us that her hunger exceeded her psychic ability and that it protected us from the same fate."

VIII

A Message at Fort Osage

We drove north to Fort Osage which was located on the Missouri River at the village of Sibley, Missouri, and it was late afternoon when we arrived at the gate by the Visitor Center. A man in Colonial military costume approached and told us that the Visitor Center had just closed for the day, but that we could walk across the park to see the log palisade and the exterior of the block house, even though the Fort itself was closed.

When we inquired if any messages had been left for Helen Stoner, he replied, "Everyone was talking about a big man who got here yesterday at closing time. He made us open the Visitor Center and take a message. We told him he could leave a message in the little box at the door, but he insisted on our taking it inside. So I'll unlock and find it for you."

He brought out an envelope and handed it to us. We thanked him for taking the extra time and he courteously offered to take more time by pointing out the big dugout canoe and the place to see a good view of the river. "This fort was established in 1808, long before Becknell traveled along here on the Trail." he explained. "It was a government-commissioned trading post on the frontier."

We were more interested at that moment in the contents of the envelope than in Fort Osage history. Opening the envelope, Helen read aloud to us the brief message inside:

See the Signal Oak at Baldwin City—The Lodge

"Baldwin City is in Kansas," Helen said. "We'll be skipping Lexington and Independence in Missouri. But my stepfather knows that I've visited the Trails Museum in Independence and already have plenty of information on both of those cities."

"It's late, but I suggest we head there immediately," said Jones. "The closer we come to Dr. Roylott the more likely we are to catch him arranging his next trap."

We followed Helen's car, driving west toward our next stop along what was becoming a very dangerous Santa Fe Trail.

IX

A Trap at Baldwin City

As we drove into Baldwin I saw a Santa Fe Trail sign, and as we continued down the road, the sign for The Lodge, which was a large log structure with porte cochere. Jones waited there in the car while I inquired about available rooms. It was then about one a.m. and the lights seemed as dim as I was.

As I opened the door to The Lodge, I fell back in surprise, almost falling off the step, because facing me immediately inside the door was a huge bear with open mouth. I regained my equilibrium as I realized it was not alive. Indeed, the entire lobby was inhabited by mounted animals. A huge Siberian bear stood at the opposite door, and the walls were covered with trophy heads of deer, antelope, and elk. "Do you have any vacancies?" I asked as I approached the desk.

A kindly-looking woman stood up and answered in the affirmative, adding, "And you don't need to worry. There aren't any bears in the rooms!" She had seen my startled double-take and was smiling at my discomfiture.

We checked in and were able to catch up on our sleep, but the next morning we had heard nothing yet from Dr. Roylott. Employees at the front desk had not received any reservation or messages, so we left word that we were at breakfast at the Black Jack Cafe next door, in case he called.

The cafe was a friendly and busy place with two rooms. The main room was decorated with designs and photos pertaining to the Santa Fe Trail. The rear dining room, reserved for non-smokers, was filled with railroad posters and memorabilia. We chose to eat there and spent considerable time perusing the walls. "We need to learn more about the Trail, Watling," said Jones "instead of these engines that supplanted it. We'll ask the waitress if there are important Trail locations still preserved near here."

Replenishing our coffee, the waitress answered with, "Oh, my yes, there's a well, there's ruts still visible out at Black Jack Park, there's an old cabin out there, there's signs all over the county about the old towns that were here before, and this was a Civil War hot spot way before the Civil War! But you need to speak to Katharine Doyenne down at the library. She's the town's historian. She'll tell you all you want to know."

After checking The Lodge for possible messages, we went there and found ninety-four-year-old Katharine Doyenne, who welcomed us eagerly. She was an attractive, sweet-faced lady who was indeed a veritable fount of information on the history of the county. She opened books and files, showed us pictures, told us stories, and when we asked about a signal oak she explained that it no longer existed, but knew her friend Dorthea Kontessa would love to take us on a tour to that spot and to the other places she'd mentioned. After placing a call she announced, "Dorthea will come to your motel tomorrow at nine. Be prepared for a great day!"

Helen then explained the reason we were looking for the Signal Oak, explaining that her stepfather, Dr. Roylott, was suggesting key places to visit along the Trail. At the mention of the name Roylott, Katharine stood up and changed her expression to an angry look. Katharine blurted, "Are you speaking of Dr. Roylott, the big man with the bushy eyebrows?"

"Yes. Was he here recently?" asked Helen.

"That man will feel the end of this cane if he ever shows up here again!" As she spoke she banged her cane on the library table, causing another librarian to come investigate the cause of the noise. "He insulted this library and all the people who work here. I've never seen such a demanding and rude individual in all my life. If this were not a public institution, I'd have him banned from the building forever."

"Yes, we've heard that he is very difficult to deal with. We are planning to meet him regarding Trail business, but we don't expect to see him here in Baldwin City," Jones said. "And if we do, we'll advise him to stay away from the library."

Helen added a few words of agreement and turned the topic away from Roylott. The conversation continued along calmer topics until we thanked Katharine and left. The Express Yourself coffee shop was a little way up the street, and there, over mochas and cookies, we discussed the plan to tour with Dorthea and find the Signal Oak.

Dorthea arrived at The Lodge promptly at nine, and we were taken on an extended tour of the county. Dorthea was an attractive, well-spoken lady with short gray hair and a dimpled chin. She was able to maintain her commentary as more of a conversation than a lecture, but her enthusiasm for the entire history of the county prolonged the tour and, because we did not want to reveal that we were interested only in the location of the Signal Oak, we had to wait until the proper opening.

"Next, I'd like to show you the Black Jack Park and the ruts of the Santa Fe Trail," she said, prompting Jones to ask casually, "Is that near the Signal Oak?"

"No, we'll go there next. But first you must see the park and the cabin here." The log cabin was an interesting collection of historical objects and information, and a little bridge in the grove of oaks led to a field that gave us an amazing view of the ruts of the Santa Fe Trail. I had not realized that there would be several deep swales and that the wagons had not always traveled in the same trail, but went in parallel, sometimes four wagons abreast. We walked in the dips, marveling that they were still in evidence at all after more than a hundred years. I got a little more practice with the camera in order to record the scene. Dorthea, who was a member of the Daughters of the American Revolution, proudly pointed out the big granite stone below the Black Jack Park sign. "There are more than a hundred of these stone markers all along the Santa Fe Trail."

Santa Fe Trail
1822-1872
Marked by the
Daughters of the American Revolution
and the State of Kansas

Beyond the park were signs commemorating the 1856 Battle of Black Jack where pro-slavery and anti-slavery forces clashed in a skirmish resulting in several deaths and exciting much publicity in the North and the South. It was the first battle fought between free and slave states before the Civil War.

We finally drove to the top of a ridge on the other side of town. A beautiful valley lay before us and next to the road was a green metal sign marking the site of the Signal Oak. The sign read

Here was a stately white oak at the time of the Civil War whose branches were used to hold signal lanterns.

Dorthea explained that when locals heard that pro-slavery raiders were on the march and burning houses along the way, they put lighted lanterns in the tree to warn distant farms of their approach.

There seemed nothing untoward about the sign or the area. We stood musing about our quest and listening to Dorthea. Then Jones noticed another sign at the edge of the clearing next to the fence. Approaching it, we focused on reading a more detailed explanation of the same events. It was Helen who made the discovery of the unusual object. "Look, there's a little green bottle tied to the branch of that tree on the other side of the fence."

She started to climb the fence, but Jones drew her back. "The dirt and leaves on the other side of the fence don't look right. There may be a hole there. Let's try farther on along the fence."

Jones was right. Testing that spot later with a rock, she found that it gave way, opening to a considerable pit. As for the tree branch, it broke almost as soon as touched, crashing down with considerable force. Helen retrieved the bottle, and as she picked it up said, "It's empty. Someone left it here as a joke or to scare away the birds."

Jones and I knew she may be concealing a real discovery, but the conversation topic was returned to the Civil War, the little bottle saved in Helen's jacket pocket, and Jones and I had to maintain our patience till the end of the tour. Dorthea did not realize that perhaps we had found a clue connected with our search and that perhaps we had almost been the intended victims of a serious accident.

After Dorthea let us off at The Lodge, Helen, Jones, and I gathered excitedly in our room and opened the bottle. It was so tiny and the neck so narrow that it did not allow extraction of the rolled paper within. But Jones found a pair of tweezers in her cosmetic bag, and with careful twisting finally removed the paper which contained the single message

Sons broke the rule at the Trailside school

"Now I see how this game works," said Jones. "Roylott is leading you on and designing cleverly laid traps intending to injure or kill. A fall into that concealed pit or a blow on the head from the weakened branch could have been fatal, but would have been construed as an accident. We definitely will follow this game and look for a way to catch him in his evil set ups."

"But now that we know there is a real plot against her, I don't think Helen should be exposed to this danger," I said. "Jones and I should probably carry on by ourselves."

"Oh, no," put in Helen. "I'm used to the way he designs these instructions. And he may plan to spy on me to be sure I'm following the game. You are in as much danger as I am. Are you sure you want to take on this project?"

I could tell that Jones was eager to continue the chase. With eyes sparkling at the challenge, she replied, "We've promised to help you, and if Watling is as keen as I am to continue, we'll say there's no stopping us. Agreed, Watling?"

I nodded as Jones put out her hand and said, "Give me your wrist and hand on it, then, for a three-way handshake of agreement."

It was done, and we set to work to decipher Roylott's note.

"I didn't think about fingerprints. I shouldn't have handled the bottle or put it into my pocket," said Helen.

"At this point, fingerprints would do no good. We will need a lot more evidence in order to charge him with a crime. He must not be far in advance of us along the Trail, and if we can find the location of the next message, and can anticipate his next trap, we could catch him in the act."

"There must've been several schools along the Trail

in early days. We'll need to find the next one along the Trail west of here," I said. "Or do you think it could be east of here. Would Roylott direct the game eastward, back toward Kansas City or Franklin?"

"I recall Dorthea saying something about a museum next to a school east of here," I said. "She'll tell us where it is."

A call was made. Dorthea seemed pleased that we were still 'Trail-ing it' and proud to state that one of her uncles had attended the little one-room school at Lanesfield. "The school is still there, and there's now a museum on the property with displays about the old one-room schools of Kansas." She was unable to escort us, but her clear directions led us along the Trail the next morning to the Lanesfield school.

Fine September sunshine on farm fields put the three of us in merry spirits as we drove along, following the county roads. Cows grazed leisurely along tree-lined fence rows, and the pastoral tranquillity made us ashamed to be in a modern automobile, stirring up a cloud of dust as we hurried to our destination.

As we pulled into the parking lot at the Lanesfield Museum, we saw a docent dressed in a long black skirt, with a white ruffled petticoat showing below the hem. Her blouse was the white high-necked, puffed-sleeve fashion of the 19th century schoolmarm. She greeted us with a smile. "Hello, I'm Laura Smilested. Welcome to the Lanesfield School. You've come at a good time.

A group of visiting third-graders has just left, so the school building is still open. You're welcome to look at it before touring the exhibits here."

We thanked her, and after a quick walk through the limestone building, which was very clean and refurbished in the proper style, we returned to the museum building near another D.A.R. marker identical to the ones we'd seen at Baldwin City. We looked at the exhibits inside the building and asked questions. Laura told us that the school was indeed directly on the Trail. "Were there any unruly students in those days?" I asked.

"There must have been a fair share," she replied. "But the teachers kept strict discipline, and we don't have any records of unruly behavior. When the wagons went by, the students were let out to watch. They ran alongside the caravan and begged for treats."

We had examined the school and the museum thoroughly and had found no answer to our riddle. "We're headed west along the Santa Fe Trail," Jones said. "Are there any other museum schools that have been restored along the Trail?"

"Oh, yes! Not a museum school, but a modern one in session today. If you're headed west on Highway 56, you'll come to the Santa Fe Trail High School west of Overbrook. It sits directly on the Trail."

That must be the one, I thought. We thanked her, hurried out to the car, and drove back through Baldwin City on Highway 56 as fast as the posted speed limit allowed. At Overbrook a mural on a large building at the edge of the road portrayed the church, an old railroad train, and a covered wagon pulled by oxen. Above them was painted in large letters

DON'T OVERLOOK OVERBROOK.

But we did have to 'overlook Overbrook' in our hurry to reach the The Santa Fe Trail High School. It was a low modern building set back from the road, displaying a sign in front. From the parking lot we saw the stone marker in front of the sign and assumed it was another D.A.R. marker similar to the ones we'd already seen. I led the way, but we made the mistake of entering the main hallway just as the passing bell between classes had rung. The tide of teenagers charging down the packed corridor was like a herd of stampeding cattle. I was knocked to the side and banged up against a locker, then shoved aside, as a dark-haired boy with baggy pants stopped to open it. "Oh, sorry," he said. "We're on our way to a pep rally. Classes are out early. Are you here for the program?"

I regained my composure, accepted his apology and asked directions to the main office. "We're doing some research and reporting about the Santa Fe Trail," Jones explained to the student receptionist. "Could you direct us to someone who might have time to talk with us?"

"Mr. Wagner is the American history teacher," she replied. "He's in the pep rally at the moment, but if you can wait a few minutes, he'll be free. I'll page him to let him know you're here."

Following the echoing cheers and the sound of band music, the herd of students re-entered the hallway, headed to lockers and to waiting buses for the trip home. A tall man coming into the office greeted us with an embarrassed smile. "Excuse the pink and green hair-do. This is Spirit Day, and I promised to spike my hair with these colors if a majority of kids turned in their term papers yesterday, before the weekend. I'm Robert Wagner. How can I help you?"

"We're trying to pick up some unusual facts about your school in connection with the Santa Fe Trail," began Jones. "Do you have a few minutes to talk to us?"

"Sure. First of all, you know we are right on the Trail itself. And did you read the marker out front? That marker is the only one along the entire Trail that was placed by the Sons, instead of the Daughters, of the American Revolution. Come along to my classroom, I'm to meet a student there and I can perhaps give you a few more facts."

Sons broke the rule. That's it, I thought. We didn't really need any more facts, just the directions to the next puzzle stop. But we introduced ourselves and chatted a few minutes, glad to excuse ourselves so that his waiting student could be accommodated. Outside, we read the marker which was as Wagner had said, placed by the Sons of the American Revolution. We searched around the sign and the grassy area near it, but found no clues pointing to our next step in the game.

We returned to the school with the idea of chatting further with Mr. Wagner. "Let's find the computer room and look for Sons of the A.R. on the Internet," suggested Helen. But Mr. Wagner was gone, the computer room was locked, and the student receptionist invited us to return the next day. "Even though it's Saturday, the computer room will be open during the morning." We thanked her and drove back to have dinner at Baldwin, planning to return the next day.

"Well, we didn't meet any dangerous traps," Helen remarked.

"Unless you count my near death by student trampling," I said.

"We're not through with the Santa Fe Trail School yet," Jones added. "We may yet discover something perilous there tomorrow."

X

The Cave at Council Grove

The next morning found us back in the hallway of the school on our way to the computer room. We had difficulty logging on to the machines because we lacked a password, and even after getting on line with the help from a student there, were unable to call up any references to the Sons. As we were about to give up or try the school library as an alternative, Mr. Wagner walked into the room with a message for us from the office. "Is Helen Stoner here? There's a message from the office saying you're to meet a Dr. Roylott in Council Grove. The secretary wrote it out for you," he said and handed Helen the paper.

"Thank you. We hardly recognized you. You look at little different from yesterday," Helen said. The transformation was amazing. He had shaved, and the pink and green was gone from his hair which lay in smooth dark waves above his wide forehead and dark eyes.

We wasted no time in returning to the car and perusing the rest of the message:

Meet me at seven a.m. day-after-tomorrow at the place where Mr. Augustini lived. S. Roylott.

The cryptic note left us very little to go on and very little time to change hotels. It was enough to hurry us back to Baldwin, check out, and drive west on the Trail again to find the town of Council Grove.

As we drove, Helen was the first to remark on Mr. Wagner's appearance. "What a handsome guy! I wish my teachers in high school had looked that good. And so tall. He's a good match for you, Sheila."

"Probably very married with an adoring wife and family," replied Jones. " And even if not, I'm through with men. They're a nuisance. And I'm too old to be in the marriage market!"

"I'd say not," objected Helen. "With your curly hair and dimples, you'll attract some gentleman who'll convince you otherwise. Don't you agree, Dora?"

"Jones has been burned by a bad experience. She's sworn off all men," I replied. "And I myself am not looking for a partner because I don't think I'll ever find one as good as my Harry who died many years ago. I'll remain a merry widow, enjoying the single life. But I'll bet you're the object of several interested swains. Isn't that so, Helen?"

Jones broke in with, "Watling, you're following lines of inquiry a little too far from our major purpose. You have been recording my cases in the proper manner up to now. Don't turn this report into a romance."

"Unnecessary details of our personal lives will be deleted, of course," I replied. "But if a romantic liaison occurs during the time of this investigation, I could perhaps market the report as a romantic novel!"

Helen laughed, but Jones sniffed, "Trash books, that's what those romances are."

"The critics may agree with you, but it's a fact that over half of all books sold are romances. You can look it up," I countered.

Helen agreed. "My lit professor said the romance novel has the distinction of being the most popular and at the same time the least respected of all literary genres. But you can't class all romance writers together. I wouldn't put the modern 'bodice rippers' in the same category with Jane Austen's books!"

The discussion ended as we approached Baldwin. We were forced to discuss dinner, time of leaving town, and whether to continue taking both Helen's and Jones' cars. We agreed we'd leave as soon as possible. And in case of emergency side trips or breakdowns, it would be best to caravan with both cars. Deciding to eat somewhere along the way, we checked out of The Lodge and were on our way west again along the Santa Fe Trail.

Our route took us through the little town of Burlingame, where nearly every business along the main street included the name of the Santa Fe Trail. We stopped for a hasty hamburger dinner at the Santa Fe Trail Cafe and were fascinated by the historic photos and charts along the walls. Behind the cash-register counter was a painting depicting both the train and the covered wagon. I climbed up on a chair to get a photo with the digital camera.

When we commented to the waitress about how wide the main street seemed to be, she explained it was made wide enough for a wagon and team to turn around in. "This is where they had a blacksmith shop and lots of the mules and horses were shod here. And you'll see up on the corner, there's a special D.A.R. marker. It's for Fannie Thompson, the woman who started the idea of putting all those markers along the Trail."

As we drove on toward Council Grove, Jones remarked, "This is really Santa Fe Trail country. Look out there on the left." High on a distant hill was the silhouette of three Indians on horses. The metal sculptures made a realistic and beautiful outline against the sunset sky. We learned later that all the major approaches to the town featured Trail silhouettes of wagons and riders.

The main street of Council Grove had maintained its early-American look with brick store fronts and Victorian street lamps. We saw a sign for Flint Hills Bed & Breakfast and felt fortunate to find vacancies available there. The hostess, Mary Lamb, a lively blonde lady wearing boots, jeans, and Indian jewelry, welcomed us into a living room decorated with sheep and lamb figurines. "Because of my last name, my friends enjoy giving me sheep, but I'm a former railroad conductor, so I prefer collecting trains," she explained.

She reached for a wall switch, and we looked up to see a miniature train mounted on a track which ran around the entire living room above window level. The little lights flashed, the whistle blew, and the tiny engine pulled the string of cars even through a tunnel built into the back of a tall bookcase. "Families with little kids really enjoy staying here," she said. We could understand that, but explained we were interested in the Santa Fe Trail.

"You've come to the right place," she said. "Follow me." In the vestibule was a table covered with brochures. "Here's the Park Service map. Look. it's almost five feet long." She snapped open the accordion-fold brochure and dangled the entire Santa Fe Trail before us. "And here's the Council Grove map. It's packed with Trail sites you'll want to visit."

She led us up the stairs where we found rooms named Kaw Indian Rest, Cowboy Corral, Eagle Nest, and finally, The Santa Fe Trail Room. Helen took first dibs on the Santa Fe Trail Room, and Jones and I chose the Eagle Nest room. Jones claimed the low narrow cot in the corner, leaving me with the huge four-poster which stood so high off the floor it was a real effort to climb up into it. There were photos of birds high on the walls, coyote pictures at eye level, and a huge turtle shell on the desk. That night I slept uneasily, and probably because I feared falling out of bed, was plagued by weird dreams. The most vivid one was of the turtle shell which seemed to be crawling toward the ceiling and talking in a squeaking voice. "Mr. Augustini, Mr. Augustini," it kept saying.

Breakfast was a grand affair including scrapple and sausage along with the eggs and fruit. Our hostess was a treasure trove of information and told about the historic sites to see in Council Grove. "You'll need three days to see it all properly," she said. But she did not remember a Mr. Augustini. We looked for his name in the phone book and called the newspaper office to inquire of the history editor there. No luck. "But there are plaques on all the houses of historic interest," Mary said. "If you do the walking tour starting along this main street, I'll bet you'll find it."

We noted a sign pointing off the main street toward "Hermit's Cave." But because buildings were the most important to us now, we decided to do the main street first. The first historic building we saw was The Last

Chance Store. It was not yet open for the day, but by reading the signs and looking in the windows, we learned that Council Grove had been the last stop for supplies for the wagons in the early days before they headed out across the plains. This was the place to assemble the wagons into caravans and elect a leader. Here was a grove of trees to supply wood for extra axles and wheel spokes. Toward the center of town was a "Post Office Oak" where departing travelers left messages with hopes of delivery by someone going back east. This was the edge of civilization, a place to say goodbye to all the comforts and to lay up supplies for the long and arduous trip to New Mexico.

At the bookstore in the center of town we asked if there was a guidebook for the historic places of Council Grove. "Oh, yes," the owner said. "And if you're driving along the whole Trail, the book you want is called *Following the Santa Fe Trail: A Guide for Modern Travelers,* by Marc Simmons. It has several pages about Council Grove. But I'm sold out right now. No matter. You just go on down this street and you'll see the covered wagon, the Madonna of the Trail, the Council Oak, the Post Office Oak, the old railroad depot, and the old jail where all the bad guys were kept. Turn off to the right and you'll see the Seth Hayes House. He was the important man in early Council Grove. Augustini? Augustini? I don't recall any Augustini. But the information in the Seth Hays House may have his name."

We walked toward the river and passed by the Hays House Restaurant, noting that it looked like a good place to have dinner later. On our walk we crossed the Neosho River Bridge and had to stop at the Madonna of the Trail statue. On a square stone base, a pioneer woman wearing a bonnet and heavy boots looks westward. In one arm she holds a baby, in the other a rifle. A young boy is clinging to her skirts. Her face shows the determination and courage of the real pioneer mother.

The Council Oak was the place where the Indians had signed an agreement to allow peaceful crossing of their lands. At the Post Office Oak I asked, "Is there a chance that Roylott could have left a note here?" The truncated bole of the tree bore no box or slit that could have concealed a message, and Jones reminded me that Roylott had said he'd meet Helen, which meant that there would be an encounter instead of a written message.

We turned off the main street and found the Seth Hays House, now a museum. Seth Hays was the great-grandson of Daniel Boone, cousin of Kit Carson, and the first white settler in Council Grove. We learned that Hays had lived here with an adopted daughter and his slave Aunt Sally, but saw no references to Augustini.

That evening we enjoyed dinner at the Hays House Restaurant. A sign said, "The Oldest Eating Establishment West of the Mississippi."

"Wait a minute," Helen said. "That was the same claim listed on the menu at the Huston Tavern in Arrow Rock."

"But notice the phrase on this menu, 'continuously operating,' said Jones. "The restaurant at Arrow Rock probably resumed only after being restored." A stone wall and the old oaken beam above the fireplace were part of the original building and kept the old western atmosphere for the diners. Upstairs was another dining area with white tablecloths and private tables, but we chose the main dining room downstairs where tables were almost filled. We were led to a table near the salad bar and were discussing the Trail and our search for Mr. Augustini, when an elderly gentleman who had over-heard part of our conversation stopped and said, "You know Augustini walked the whole Trail from here to New Mexico."

He was as gnarled and knobby as the cane he carried. He had a long drooping mustache and hair that reached to his shoulders, but he stood erect and was eager to impart knowledge of the Trail. We invited him to sit with us and tell us where Mr. Augustini's house was.

"No house. When he was here he lived in a cave! It's just a few blocks from here. Called Hermit's Cave. He was born in Italy and they say he lived in caves in Canada before coming here. His people were high-class Italian nobles, but he was kind of a religious hermit, a mystic."

"Was his cave fixed up like a house" I asked.

"Too darn small. It's a little tiny hole in the cliff. You can go look at it. But he didn't stay there very long. He joined a wagon train going to New Mexico, to the Las Vegas area. Probably found a bigger cave. But they say he performed some miraculous cures and there's a shrine to him up on some mountain there."

So our search for Augustini had ended. He was remembered mostly as The Hermit, rather than Giovanni Maria Augustini; hence our difficulty in finding information. We discussed the possibility of going to the cave ahead of the appointed time. But it was getting late. Darkness made the prospect an unwise course of action. So it was back to the B&B and another restless night in the big four-poster bed. Instead of the turtle, I dreamed of caves with big stalactites in the shape of crosses and stalagmites in the shape of cowled monks.

The next morning the weather was fair and the cave was within walking distance, so we made our way up the street following the signs. One vehicle, a black pickup, was parked at the curb near the path marked "To the Cave." We were directed down the steep slope toward the river. The area had been preserved with stone steps and clearly marked. Just before the path turned toward the cave, a young man came running up the slope on the path from the river.

"Stop! Don't go into the cave!" He was breathless and red-faced. He carried a pair of binoculars in one hand and his coat in the other. "I'm Eddie Robledo.

Are you Helen? Your sister and your Aunt Lillian sent me. I've been trying to find you. I've been watching from that tree over there. A man kept going in and out with wires and..." His explanations came in short confusing statements that left us amazed. We waited for him to catch his breath and looked around in search of Roylott.

"Look, " he said. "There's a wire showing up there. Don't touch it. I'll try to hook it with this branch." And as he did so, a huge boulder crashed down just inside the entrance to the cave. The noise echoed and a cloud of dust puffed up out of the entrance. Helen and I stood stunned, but Jones began running up the path toward the street calling, "Get him!"

She had guessed that the black pickup truck parked at the top of the path belonged to Roylott and that he had waited to see the results of the planned trap. We followed her up the path, but were too late to get a license plate number as the truck was already turning the corner and zooming away at top speed.

Jones was first to express regret that she had not noted the license plate of the black pickup. "My Sherlockian talent is slipping," she said.

Gratitude for our escape and amazement at the appearance of our rescuer kept us at the cave while we recovered and asked how Eddie Robledo came to be our saving angel. He brushed his dark brown hair away from his forehead and stared at us with the darkest eyes I'd ever seen. He kept saying, "Wow! I can't believe this. You're Helen. You look like Julia. Wow! What a close call!"

He explained that he and his brother Raoul worked as gardeners at the abbey where Julia Stoner was a nun. Although there was almost complete silence within the abbey, Julia and Raoul had become friends as they worked together in the abbey gardens. The letters from Aunt Lillian were a great worry. Julia had confided her concerns about Roylott's Trail game and begged him to find her sister Helen and stop her from going any farther. Raoul had convinced Eddie that he could better afford the time away from his job, and sent him to find Helen. They studied maps of the Trail and noted the towns along the route.

"Julia said you probably had been gone a week and that you'd be past Kansas City. The map shows that Council Grove was the major stop for the wagons, so I've been looking up and down this town. Last night at the restaurant I saw a big man who looked like the description Julia gave me. I followed him. I saw the motel where he stayed last night, and waited till he came out this morning."

"I commend you as an excellent sleuth," said Jones. "You deserve credit as a good 'shadow man.'"

Eddie smiled and thanked her for the compliment, but regretted he also had neglected to note the license plate number on the black pickup. He poked at the tangle of wires and rocks to make sure there were no other dangers, and we hurried to inform the police. Here was definite criminal intent. We surmised that Roylott had planned the blow for early in the morning before any other tourists would be about and that the appointment he'd made clearly focused on Helen as a victim.

But although the officer sent someone to investigate the "Crime scene" and radioed the Highway Patrol to pursue the black pickup, he discouraged our having much success because Eddie, as the only witness, was unable to identify the criminal other than that he wore a dark coat and stocking cap. With no license plate data, the Patrol would have a difficult time stopping every black pickup truck.

Over lunch at the Hays House we discussed the dilemma. "One thing we know," I remarked. "Roylott figured that that rock would end the game. There will be no clues here to direct us to the next stop."

"If he learns that we escaped the trap, he will try again," said Jones. "Remember he gave the previous instruction in a phone message, and I look for him to do so again."

"But how does he know where to find us?" asked Helen. "How can he tell we escaped?"

"According to the brochure, there are only two motels and two B&B's in Council Grove," said Jones. "Simple process of elimination would locate us."

Jones was proven right again, as always. When we returned to the B&B we found that Roylott had left another message and assumed we would continue to follow the game along the Trail. Mary handed us the written message.

One spring has diamonds and cattle. The other is lost.

XI

The Springs and A Specter

Jones responded quickly. Pulling out the accordion-fold map, she said, "Look here. These are the next sites of importance listed on the map. Highway 56 generally follows the Trail, but these two sites are away from the road."

"I don't know about Lost Spring," said Mary, "But Diamond Spring is on private property. I think the rancher usually allows visitors."

"It behooves us to go there as soon as possible. We were close behind Roylott this time, and if we base our speculation on what happened at Baldwin City, he will be leaving only messages, not dangerous snares for us to fall into. He needs time to prepare his evil work, and I believe these next two stops are distractions only."

"I wish we could guess what that next stop will be and jump ahead to that site on the Trail," I said.

"If he's trying to make time on the road, the next major town on 56 is McPherson. After that there are several crossings used by the wagons in the old days. A marked camp or stage station could be a possibility."

So we planned to go to the springs first, get directions to the next stop, and perhaps split up with Eddie and Helen driving on ahead to look for the black pickup on the main roads.

"I'll drive for you, Helen," Eddie said. "My jalopy barely made it this far. If we leave it here and ride in your car, we'll have much better chance of getting there."

So, after checking out of the B&B it was off on the Trail again. Jones, contrary to her usual policy, drove five miles above the speed limit, while I navigated us along the county roads toward Diamond Spring. The day was warm, the air very dry, and Helen's car came behind at a distance that allowed avoiding the worst of the dust.

Up a gravelly hill, the road turned and passed by a closed metal gate. The square arch above it said DIAMOND CREEK RANCH. Not knowing the name of the owner, we had not called ahead, and there was no name or phone number on the gate, so we parked the cars, climbed the bars, and started down the lane toward the ranch house. The sun had heated the road and the air above it to stifling, and our progress was slow in spite of our eagerness to see the spring.

About half a mile along the lane, a young boy wearing glasses, a red tank top, and jeans, came running up the bank from a ranch house. He pointed the way, as if anticipating our question and said it was O.K. to visit. The gate had been shut because of moving cattle. "Do you have a cup?" he asked.

When we replied in the negative he ran back down toward the house, saying he'd meet us at the spring. The lane curved behind a huge barn near another ranch house, and under some huge trees was a stock tank filled with water, a low fountain pipe bubbling up in the center. A big brown cow lifted its dripping nose from the tank and ambled away. Nearby was another D.A.R. marker. A sign, erected by the Judds and the Santa Fe Trail Association said

Jones Spring was renamed Diamond Spring for its sparkling clear water. It was a campsite, water hole, and trading post, and the first wagon train stop west of Council Grove. In 1863 the Yeager Gang killed the storekeeper, wounded his wife, and burned the buildings.
The post office was moved to Six Mile Crossing.

We immediately plunged our arms into the cold water and began to wash the sweat from our faces. The boy we had talked to earlier rode up on his bicycle and handed us a cup. "Go ahead and drink, right where it bubbles up," he said. Jones expressed doubt about using the same trough as a Hereford, but after tasting the water, gulped down more and refilled the cup, passing it on to us. "Delicious," she proclaimed.

Helen stood near Eddie's shoulder as he bent down to wet his face, and with a giggle, pushed his head completely under the water. He roused and began splashing her, and as she ran, chased her with his cupful.

"Kids!" sniffed Jones. "We need to be more serious and begin looking for any indications pointing us onward." After an interval of searching in the immediate area and finding nothing, we walked back to the cars, sorry to have the quenched thirst and the cool water evaporate away so quickly.

Helen and Eddie drove on toward McPherson on 56 looking for Roylott, with the plan that we'd meet at the Best Western motel there, while Jones and I scouted out Lost Spring. More county roads, more dust, railroad tracks with a long freight train, and two stops to ask directions finally brought us to a sign beside the road designating it "Old Lost Spring." White words on the green metal provided more of the tragic history of the area: an Indian battle northwest of the spring and the graves of seventeen cowboys who had perished in a blizzard. Two hundred or more wagons would camp in a circle here.

The spring was quite close to the road in a shady grove, but the water trickled too slowly for scooping it up without a cup. Farther downstream, the creek was lined with watercress, and the sun, shining through the thick leaves above, dappled the water with sparkles and made the grove a restful respite from the hot roads. We sat down to rest and I was tempted to lie back and close my eyes under the leafy canopy, but Jones again emphasized the urgency of our quest and roused me to look for a clue or message that would direct us onward. We searched diligently, especially in the branches of the trees above eye level, without success. But as we returned to the car, we saw an empty sodapop can, fitted over the top of a fence post. Removing it we saw the note within: A scrawl on the paper said

THE OTHER TAMPA

"Tampa? We've got to get a more detailed map," Jones said. "But the day is wearing on, and we'd better meet the kids in McPherson first, and find out if they have learned anything."

We arrived in McPherson and checked in just as they arrived. They told us they'd been driving farther west on 56 looking for Roylott's pickup, but to no avail. In the Frontier Restaurant near the motel we told them about Lost Spring and showed them the Tampa note.

"We're really learning a lot of history," Helen said. "Even though I'd studied the Trails in American history, our going along this Santa Fe Trail is like re-living history. In the movies you hear about Indian battles, but this trip brings out the other dangers the early travelers faced. Blizzards, renegades, and their search for water, make our danger seem silly by comparison."

A man sitting with his wife in a booth near us came over and said, "Excuse me. Are you interested in the Santa Fe Trail? We're on our way out to our ranchito. The ruts of the Santa Fe Trail are visible on our property. We'd like to have you join us for our campfire there tonight." They were Steve and Linda Smithers who lived and worked in McPherson but owned some old homestead property out on the Trail. "We bought the land mainly because it's a Trail site. We enjoy going out on weekends and puttering around. We're trying to plant more native grasses and restore the area to its original condition."

Jones frowned and muttered something about a planned meeting elsewhere, but she was outvoted by the three of us, and after our meal we followed them to the Smithers Ranchito.

The late afternoon sun shone on little sunflowers along the road, and at the Ranchito glorified the fields where they nodded in abundance. We drove in past an abandoned farmhouse and parked in a grove of trees where a circle of stones marked the firepit. Linda led us through the fields and around a pond, then to the top of a small hill where we could see the ridges and troughs of the old wagon road. "Ruts always show up better in the late afternoon or early morning," she explained. We were dazzled.

Steve Smithers had put folding chairs around the firepit, and Linda let down the tailgate of their van to reveal an urn of coffee and a dishpan full of popcorn. The next surprise was the big guitar Steve pulled out and began to tune. He had come directly from work to the restaurant and was still wearing a business suit and tie, but he donned a big black western hat as a nod to the setting and occasion. Linda must have had time to dress in western pants and boots, and her dark hair complemented the white western shirt she wore.

Steve began playing familiar tunes so we could all sing-along. Then he followed with some Mexican ballads. The sun went down; the shadows deepened. The songs became more soulful. An owl gave a wavering cry from a distant barn. "That's tecolotito, the little owl," said Eddie, and he sang in Spanish as Steve played.

Tecolotito morado, pajaro madrugador
Me prestaras tus alitas para ir a ver a mi amor
(Little purple owl, early rising bird lend me your
wings so I can go to see my love.)

As he sang he looked tenderly at Helen. His dark eyes and olive skin contrasted with his white shirt. His dark coat was threadbare, missing several buttons, and his low shoes looked as if they'd been worn for too many

Sundays, but he resembled some handsome Spanish gypsy with a melodious voice. We were charmed, and Helen especially so.

The fire was dying down but the light still shone on the faces around it as night darkened the grove. I sat facing Steve as he played and all at once became aware of a figure in the darkness beyond him. Had a neighbor heard the music and crept up to join us? I nudged Jones and nodded toward the dark figure. She looked at me, then across at Steve, and not noticing anything, looked back at me questioningly.

Linda threw another log onto the fire and as it blazed up, the darkness beyond our circle seemed darker by contrast, but I could distinguish that the figure was a woman wearing a long dress and a black bonnet. "Come join us," I called out. The others turned to follow my gaze. Eddie stood up and walked toward the trees, as if to invite the newcomer. But there was no one there!

Steve took a flashlight from his vehicle and probed the darkness. "Probably a deer. They've been wandering through here lately."

"I guess I'm seeing shadows," I stated meekly. But I was shaking inwardly with the realization that I had seen the same Lucille phantom that had appeared to me at the Irish pub in Kansas City! Do ghosts leave their venue to pursue the living on their travels? Why was I the only one to see this spectre? These questions whirled around in my head as the music continued. I was glad that the fire was dying down again, to prevent anyone's noticing my agitated state, and that the singing prevented any questions arising from the group.

Just as I had not related my experience at Rivercene, neither did I dare confide in Sheila Jones regarding this ghostly experience. Her ultra rational outlook did not allow for visions, specters, or other-worldly experiences. She could not accuse me of imbibing alcoholic spirits this time. Her reaction would be to surmise that I was going daffy, so I laughed off my invitation to the "stranger" as a joke. But now I felt that our Santa Fe Trail journey held more than history lessons or the pursuit of an evil stepfather.

XII

The Vault and The Hikers

The next morning we purchased a big book of Kansas county maps at the superstore near the motel and headed for Tampa. The little town lay directly on the Trail. On the north side near the cemetery we found the marker and began looking for a clue directing us to the next stop. The sign was interesting, being the only one we had seen that actually included the phrase "purchased from the Indians." Against a fence post nearby was a sign advertising a restaurant.

Butch's Diner.
You can Bank on us for a Good Meal

Eddie suggested that he and Helen could check out Butch's Diner while Jones and I did more searching at the

Trail corner near the sign. So they left with the plan to meet us there within the hour. Finding nothing near the sign we walked across the road to the cemetery to search for gravestones that may date from Trail days. An elderly lady who had been putting flowers on one of the graves was leaving as we entered the gate. We asked her if she'd recommend Butch's Diner for our lunch.

"Oh my yes," she said. "But you'd better get there early. They serve dinner in the middle of the day and are closed in the evening. It's quite a place. It used to be a bank and the kitchen is located in the bank vault." We thanked her and after a short stroll among the graves, left to find Butch's Diner.

It was a short drive because we were within four blocks of the restaurant. But as we drove up, we noticed a crowd of people and a sheriff's car in front. Something was wrong! We parked as close as possible and walked through the crowd into the restaurant where we found a scene of intense stress. The waitpeople were crowded around a big door, which proved to be the door to the vault. The manager, a burly man with a sweaty face and hair that stood out on the sides of his head, was frantically turning the combination dial on the door, trying to open it. Eddie stood by him offering advice and repeating, "Let me try it. Let me try! Helen, we'll get you out." The sheriff's deputy was talking on the phone apparently trying to reach the owner to find out who had the combination to the vault.

Here, Sheila Jones displayed her mastery of the situation. Parting the crowd with an air of authority, she approached the huge door and reaching high to the right side, began lifting the various pans that were hanging there, until she removed a collander revealing a piece of paper with the numbers of the combination written on it!

She dialed the combination, pulled the handle, and the heavy door swung open to reveal the chubby cook in a white apron, and Helen, both with smiles of relief on their faces.

It was Eddie who suddenly realized that we should be giving chase to the culprit who had shut them in. It was Roylott himself! Eddie ran to the deputy, who was hanging up the phone and began telling him who had closed the vault, expecting him to give chase immediately. "The man who closed the safe went that way!" he shouted. But to his chagrin everyone seemed to look upon the situation as a big joke! Even Helen and the cook were laughing. The "safe kitchen" was not air tight and they had been in no danger. "I hope you were making more soup in there," the manager said. "There are people waiting for their dinner."

Only Jones and Eddie wore stern looks, and Eddie began to explain how the situation had arisen. They had entered the diner and expressed interest in the unusual decor. The manager invited them to explore. First, answering Eddie's question, he directed him to the "president's office" behind a curtain where the restrooms were. As Eddie came back into the main dining area, he saw a big man in a black vest closing the door to the vault. He ran out the side door. Yes, he said, the man had a white mustache and bushy black eyebrows. The manager had yelled at him to come back, but it was too late. The lock had clicked and the door was sealed. Realizing that Helen had been locked inside, Eddie's first concern was for her rescue, and his reaction was to try to open the door. A crowd gathered, the sheriff was called, and during the frantic attempts to open the safe, the culprit had vanished.

As calm was being restored to the diner, the owner, Butch himself, arrived and complimented Jones on her rational decision to look under the pans for the combination numbers. "Most locked doors have a key concealed within sight distance, and as long as the safe was now a kitchen I knew there would be no need to hide the combination at a distance," said Jones.

Attempting to pursue the culprit would be useless. He would by now be far down the road. The aroma of fried chicken pervaded the dining room, and we decided that the wisest course to follow would be to sit down and enjoy a good meal. "We can bank on it," laughed Helen. Before we left, Butch presented her with a souvenir, a blue tee shirt bearing the inscription in white letters "Butch's Diner."

Our map showed that the Trail went parallel to the

highway and south of it. Rather than try to find the crossings on the Arkansas River, we decided to head for the site that was nearer the highway, believing that Roylott in his haste would follow 56 farther west. The next town was Lyons, and a few miles west of it we saw a park with a huge white cross commemorating Father Padilla and Coronado's Expedition. They had come looking in the north country for the fabled Quivira in the sixteenth century. We stopped to read the signs and marker. "Wow! I didn't know Coronado got this far east," said Eddie.

As we were studying the printed information, we heard singing, and looked around to see a group of women hiking along the side of the road toward us.

We want to visit Old Franklin
Leaving from Old Santa Fe.
We'll do it without a wagon
Hiking it all the way.

There were five women who looked to be in their sixties. Four of them approached laughing, and introduced themselves. The fifth woman had crossed the road to pet a horse that leaned over the fence there. A woman in a battered blue straw hat said she was the Trail Boss. "We're hiking the entire Santa Fe Trail from Santa Fe, New Mexico, to Franklin, Missouri," she announced. "We go out each spring and fall and get a little farther each year, picking up where we left off last time. We've been at it for a long time, but when we finish we think we'll qualify for the Guinness Book of World Records as being the oldest and the slowest to walk the Trail!"

"And do you camp out at night? How do you manage without going back for a car?" we asked.

"We stay in motels. We always have two cars. We drive both ahead to our ten-mile destination, then come back in one and hike to the first car."

"You hike ten miles every day?"

"Usually five before lunch and five afterwards. We feel we can keep it up for five days, at least. We like to spend that much time on the Trail because we're so far from home now that it takes a day to drive here."

"Do you hike only along the main roads?"

"Oh no, we try to avoid the highway. We've been hiking north of here, but because the Trail crosses the highway near here, we had to hike this little bit along the road."

A second woman broke in with, " Most of the Trail here in Kansas has been plowed into farms, but we have a book of maps showing where it originally went, so we try to hike on the nearest county road."

A third woman added, "Except when we were in New Mexico and Oklahoma. We got permission from some of the ranchers and were able to hike in the actual ruts of the Trail." She took off her back pack and sat down to drink from her canteen.

The others did likewise, and we continued our questions. "This is a pretty big project. What got you started in the first place?"

"Various reasons," said Trail Boss. "But hers is the most dramatic." She pointed at a neatly dressed woman wearing a white turtle-neck shirt. "Tell them, Phyllis," she said.

"I knew nothing about the Trail until one night I had a strange dream. I dreamed I was riding in a covered wagon behind a pair of big oxen. It was so vivid. I could smell the dust and hear the whips popping.

"Someone was walking along beside the wagon. That's when I realized that I should be the one walking instead of riding. I woke up with the words in my mind that I wanted to hike the Santa Fe Trail!"

"She found us at one of the meetings of the Santa Fe Trail Association," said Trail Boss. "And we invited her to join the project."

"I'm Carolyn," broke in another woman. "I joined the group later, but I'm going to hike the part I missed at the beginning. Have some almonds?" She held out a bag of goodies. Another woman who had remained standing said, "Come on. We've got to get in our ten miles. The car is way up at Lyons."

"Judy keeps us on schedule," said Carolyn. "But where are you from? Are you driving to all the Trail sites?"

"We're partly following a trip that was mapped out for us. But we've lost track of our leader," I said. "What was your last Trail stop? Did you notice a man in a black pickup passing you anywhere along the road?"

Phyllis said, "No, we were at Ralph's Ruts at our last stop."

Judy added, "That's an interesting place. A man named Ralph Hathaway has preserved a big square of land where the Trail crossed his property."

"Did you notice any signs, messages, or envelopes that may contain a note?" Jones asked.

"There was a little green bottle on the rail above the gate, but it looked like a medicine bottle. We picked up some cans and other trash, but the bottle was too high to reach."

Judy called to the woman who was petting the horse. "Come on, Jennifer. It's getting late." And the group said their goodbyes and walked on down the road, singing the next verse of their Trail Song.

San Miguel del Vado
Tecolote too
Las Vegas and old Fort Union
Remember the gray and the blue

"Onward to Ralph's Ruts." said Jones. And we were off on our next stage of the game.

XIII

The Haunted Museum at Great Bend

A sign directing us onto a road north of the highway led us to a gate and a D.A.R. marker on the east side of the road. Beyond it we could see the beautiful definition of swales in the field. We began searching for the green bottle, but could not find it. Then we saw a man in coveralls wearing a gray cap, walking toward us. It was Mr. Hathaway himself, who offered to take us out onto the field. We accepted and found ourselves listening to the story he told about a terrible massacre that had occurred there in 1867. The caravan had been traveling single file. The Indians had cut off the wagons at the tail end, killed two people, stole the goods they were transporting, and set fire to the prairie, preventing the other wagons from helping the victims. Our search for the little green bottle seemed trivial in comparison. Hathaway said he hadn't noticed any bottles or messages, but explained, "If you're headed west on the Trail, you'll come to Pawnee Rock. That's where the travelers left messages in the old days. They carved their names on the rock there. Of course, it's a preserved site now, and no carving allowed, but if you're in a game where you're looking for messages, I'd say that's a likely spot."

We thanked him and started walking toward the cars when he called after us, "Say, are you museum buffs? Course, if you're heading west, you've already missed the good one at Lyons. It has Santa Fe Trail and Quivira Indian stuff. Coronado too!"

Jones stopped and explained that due to time restraints we'd probably have to forego the Lyons museum. Hathaway nodded and added, "Talked to a fellow who came by here yesterday. He was headed for Great Bend to see the museum there. That's on west of here."

"Was he a big man with white mustache?" Jones asked. "Did you notice if he drove a black pickup?"

"I believe so," Hathaway answered. "Friend of yours?"

"Yes, we're trying to catch up to him. We'll try to find him there. Thank you very much." Jones added privately to me, "That's probably the destination listed in the missing green bottle."

The museum was about to close by the time we arrived in Great Bend and asked directions to find it. A kindly docent, learning that we were interested in the Santa Fe Trail called to two gentlemen who were working in a rear office. They were Bob and Ray of the Trail, a pair of history buffs who did a weekly radio show featuring the Santa Fe Trail in the area of Great Bend. Their eager dedication was immediately manifest in their invitation to tour us to the Trail sites, but we asked to tour the museum first, and walked into the various rooms looking for special displays that might contain a message.

The Santa Fe Trail section contained interesting displays of maps and artifacts collected from the Trail. A huge buffalo head was mounted on the wall above them. There seemed to be no message left there, but we lingered quite a while perusing the collection.

The museum focused on other eras in addition to Trail history. A large section was devoted to World War II and the local veterans who had served their country. Jones noticed a piano in one of the rooms and investigated to see if it was a mechanical player piano. She found that it was not and returned to the Santa Fe Trail displays.

I drifted off to a corner to look at an elaborate doll collection. The dolls were dressed in costumes of different countries and eras. I noticed especially the 19th Century frontier doll who wore a long brown dress with white apron, big boots, and bonnet. She looked like a miniature version of the Madonna of the Trail statue we'd seen earlier.

Suddenly Helen called out, "Come here and look at the switchboard!"

We found her by a display featuring a mannequin in 50's dress wearing a headset and seated at an old fashioned switchboard with its multiple sockets and cords. The mannequin operator held one cord in her hand as if to plug it into the board to make a connection for a phone call. But the startling thing about the display was that the top of the board was covered with pieces of paper bearing notes and comments from various people regarding the museum or messages to other vacationers.

The docent came hurrying up to the display also and explained, "Oh yes, this is our message board. A visitor last year put a note on it for the rest of his family who he knew was coming the next day. His mother used to be a switchboard operator at the old hotel here. The idea caught on because everybody thought the switchboard was an appropriate place for messages, so we encourage visitor comments here."

Helen had removed one large piece of paper and held it out to us. It contained, scrawled in pencil, in Roylott's handwriting, the lines

Helen—Be careful at Pawnee Rock

"Pawnee Rock?" said Helen. "That's the place Mr. Hathaway told us about, the place where the early travelers left their names carved on the cliff." We agreed

106

that would be our next destination.

Because it was past closing time, we returned to the lobby and told Bob and Ray we didn't have time to schedule any tours with them, but we'd like to buy a few cassette tapes of their radio programs. The lights were being turned off in the main part of the museum and only the lobby was lighted as the docent wrapped our tapes for us. Suddenly we heard piano music coming from the back rooms. "Do you have more than one piano?" asked Jones. "There must be a mechanical one back there."

"Oh no. That's our resident ghost. I'll turn the lights back on and it will stop. We haven't heard it in a long time. One of you must be a channeler or a "fey" spirit as they say," she said laughing. She switched on the light, and Jones immediately walked back to the room with the piano. The old upright instrument was silent and the lid over the keys was shut. Jones pushed the piano away from the wall and lifted the lid on the top. So convinced was she that there must be a mechanism other than the hammers and strings that she stood examining it for several minutes.

We gathered around also, and it was Eddie who noticed the doll lying under the piano bench. He picked it up and handed it to the docent who said, "How did this get here? It's supposed to be in the doll-collection room." I looked closer and recognized the doll I had admired earlier. But I had seen no one else in that room and I certainly hadn't touched any of the dolls. "I'll put it back," I said. "I think I know where it goes." Sure enough, there was the blank space where the doll had stood. Back at the lobby desk I asked, "Does the ghost ever move objects around?"

"Not that I recall," she said. "But this is the first time in a long time that the piano has played with no one there; so who knows what other ghosts may have returned! We plan to get a night watchman soon, and I tell you I wouldn't want that job."

We took our tapes and, thanking Bob and Ray and the docent, headed for a motel. Knowing that Jones would have a logical explanation for the invisible piano player, I asked her what she thought about the strange phenomenon. "Someone turned on a piano music tape," she said. "Museums in small towns cater to only a few people because most tourists are headed for the larger cities. Therefore, any museum that can claim to be haunted would offer a special attraction. I believe that if we could investigate the piano area more thoroughly we'd find a tape player with recorded sound effects." I wanted to suggest going back on the morrow to check out that theory, but knew that she would pooh pooh that idea, so I made no response. Exposure of that little deception was not worth the trouble compared to our larger goal.

XIV

Accusation at Fort Larned

The next day found us driving down the Trail again headed for the Pawnee Rock. Jones put one of the Bob & Ray Trail cassettes into the tape player, and we listened as we rode along. We had picked the one about the Forts, and the dialogue began like this:

BOB: Well, Ray, you said last time you'd tell us about the forts along the Santa Fe Trail. Were there a lot of them?

RAY: At one time there were as many as eleven. Kansas had the most. There were six in Kansas. Of course, most of the length of the Trail is in our state, so that explains why there were more here.

BOB: I suppose many of them are no longer in existence. Have any of them been preserved or restored?

RAY: Oh, yes, Bob. Fort Leavenworth is still an army post today, and Fort Larned is beautifully restored, as is Bent's Fort in Colorado.

BOB: Were they built during the Civil War?

RAY: Most were established before the Civil War in order to protect travelers on the Trail. Army escorts accompanied the wagon trains through hostile Indian territory. They were supply stations also. Fort Union in New Mexico was the supply depot for the whole Southwest.

Here I interrupted the tape to remind Jones that we were nearing Pawnee Rock. "I suspect Dorthea's prediction is coming true," I said.

"What prediction was that?" asked Jones.

"That we'll become 'Trail junkies,' real history addicts. They say it grows on you if you spend much time on the Trail."

"We can't lose sight of our real purpose. We'll eventually catch Roylott in his nefarious scheme."

The little village of Pawnee Rock was not far down the road and the rock itself was only a few blocks off the highway. The rock face rose abruptly above the plain, but the rear of the massive landmark was a gradual ascent with a road, allowing us to drive up to the top where there was a stone shelter and a tall monument. Jones read the marker and remarked that for once the inscription mentioned the women as well as the men who traveled on the Santa Fe Trail.

We climbed the stairs to the top of the stone shelter and were afforded a view of the plain stretching away to the highway, the village, and beyond. Eddie called our attention to a string of white tanks on wheels along a lane in the distance, looking like a miniature wagon train.

"A strange coincidence," said a voice. "Those are containers for ammonia fertilizer, but they do look like a string of wagons at this distance." We looked around to see a man in a rust colored jacket sitting at the corner holding a book. Helen drew back in worried surprise, remembering the warning note. But Jones approached him and asked about the book he held.

"It's the diary of one of the first American women to travel the Trail," he said. "Have you heard what Susan Magoffin wrote about this place in 1846?"

Because we replied in the negative and expressed an interest, he read us a passage telling that the wagon train she was traveling in with her wealthy trader husband had stopped here. Her husband stood atop the rock on guard while she cut her name into the rock alongside the others she saw there. But, "It was not done well, for fear of Indians made me tremble all over," she wrote. "And I hurried it over in any way."

"The names are long gone," said the man. "And this entire rock is not as high as formerly because the top was quarried for rock long ago."

We introduced ouselves and discovered that he was Marc Simmons, the author of the book we had been looking for. We asked him if he had a copy in his car, but he did not. Then we asked him if there could be a place where modern travelers might leave notes and he replied again in the negative, adding, "The D.A.R. marker at the base of the rock is almost hidden by lilac bushes. If a person wanted to hide something, it would certainly stay hidden there."

We thanked him and hurried down the slope. Eddie pulled the stiff branches of the bush away from the front of the monument, and there was a paper with Roylott's handwriting.

Helen—Good info about the Trail at the Trail Center

We were soon back on the road headed for Larned and the Trail Center. "That Mr. Simmons seemed very knowledgeable," Helen said. " A nice-looking intelligent man. He looked like a writer. I'll bet he's doing another book or an article about the Trail."

Jones replied. "Let's listen to more information about the forts." We missed the turn because we were again absorbed in the Bob and Ray tape, but stopped and turning back on the correct road, we were soon in view of the Santa Fe Trail Center and museum. Inside was an interesting way to follow the Trail by going from room to room while progressing from Franklin, Missouri, to Santa

Fe, New Mexico. First, just inside the door was a huge wooden two-wheeled cart. Information was posted there about the Mexican traders who brought hides, mules, and silver to the States. I had thought mostly about the traders going from Missouri to Santa Fe to sell their goods, and this display reminded us that the Trail was a road of two-way commerce. Santa Fe was originally a northern capital of a province of Spain, and the Santa Fe Trail was actually a highway between nations.

I was admiring a huge covered freight wagon when Jones called, "Look, Watling. Here's a hansom cab of the kind referred to in the Sherlock Holmes stories. As we stood admiring the shiny black coach, another museum visitor, who had circulated through the rooms in the opposite direction, joined us and remarked, "This is a great museum. And there are buildings outside also. A schoolhouse and even an underground sod shanty."

We completed the circuit of the rooms and were about to visit the other buildings, but the door was blocked with a sign: OUTDOOR EXHIBITS TEMPORARILY CLOSED. We browsed in the gift shop, still searching for clues to our next stop and looked at the books. Eddie asked which Trail book was the most popular, and bought Marian Russell's *Land of Enchantment* for Helen on the clerk's recommendation. It was written by a woman who had traveled the Trail many times with the wagon trains in the early days.

As we left the building, not having found any clues to our next step in the game, Jones noticed two police cars parked at the farther end of the lot, a Sheriff's and a State Trooper's car. She ran to the far end of the building and saw the officers talking with some museum personnel near the sod house. Re-entering the museum, she went through the closed exit and discovered the cause of the trouble. When she re-joined us she explained that the museum personnel had discovered early that morning that someone had tampered with the wires to the interior lights of the sod house, but had escaped before completing whatever vandalism had been intended. "Roylott again," she proclaimed. " That explains why there is no note to the next stage of the game. The next closest Trail site is Fort Larned. It behooves us to go there immediately."

Fort Larned is a National Historic Site. The limestone buildings around the huge parade ground contain among other structures, a museum, soldiers' quarters, kitchen, supply room, and auditorium and book store. We watched a film in the auditorium and toured the buildings looking for a message. Eddie hurried ahead of us looking into display cases, poking his hand into cannon barrels, and searching the shelves in the supply store. He disappeared to scout the outside area and after about two hours we gave up and returned to browse in the book store. I bought the Magoffin diary book that we'd heard about at Pawnee Rock, titled *Down the*

Santa Fe Trail and Into Mexico. We left the building and headed for the parking lot.

Suddenly Eddie came running across the parade ground, chased by a soldier in a blue Civil War uniform. "Stop! He took something out of the Conestoga wagon," he shouted.

Stopping in front of us, Eddie turned and said, "No! This is a message for us." And he held out a paper on which the only words were

The next fort

The soldier, who was a museum guard, looked puzzled. Then realizing that the paper was not a part of the old wagon display, apologized but added, "Our exhibits are very old and fragile. Please don't climb on them."

"What is the next fort?" Eddie asked.

"Fort Dodge, near Dodge City," he replied. "It's not a National Park site, but you can visit the little museum there. The main buildings are now a home for veterans."

We thanked him and left for that goal.

XV

Shootout at Dodge City

Fort Dodge at first looked like a series of ordinary buildings set back from the road, but when we drove in we realized that some of the buildings had been part of the original fort. The "Sutler's Store" was still there and a white two-story Colonial house with columns across the front. It was called the "Custer House." We drove past the veterans' apartments where an elderly gentleman waved to us from his wheelchair on the front porch. We found the library-museum building and anticipated a long search for our next instruction note, but were pleasantly surprised to see an envelope with Helen's name lying next to the visitor register book where we signed our names.

She opened it eagerly and found a ticket for the show in Dodge City at the Long Branch Saloon on

Front Street. The docent, a kindly lady with silver hair, explained that Front Street and Boot Hill were the tourist center of Dodge City. "The buildings have been rebuilt to look like the original town. You may find that it looks more like a movie set or an amusement park, but the museum there has some very interesting items. You'll enjoy the gunfight skit in front of the Saloon, and the show inside is worth seeing too," she added.

But after we talked about heading there immediately, she told us we should drive back to enter the city on the main road. "You need to see the Cowboys on the hill. It's a huge metal sculpture on the overlook. From there you'll have a view of one of the largest feedlots you've ever seen. It's quite a sight."

We strolled quickly through the exhibits, pausing just long enough to appear interested while concealing our hurried anticipation of Front Street. Eddie and Helen left before Jones and I did, however, and Jones seemed disturbed when she discovered they had left. "We'll catch them at the Cowboys on the hill," I said.

The Cowboys were a silhouette sculpture of several men on horses, making a very impressive outline against the western sky. But I expressed my disapproval of the smell of the huge feed lot where we could see thousands of cows in close quarters in their pens below us. Jones reminded me, "They've had a relatively pampered life, and will die quickly. Tonight you will appreciate their contribution to your steak dinner. I dare say you will enjoy the smell and taste of your filet mignon at the restaurant."

Helen and Eddie had already left the hill and Jones explained her concern regarding the Saloon show. "Do you remember the note you filed, Watling, in your Ingenious Murders File about the movie shoot-outs? As I recall, it was treated in the *Stone of the Sun* book by S.R. Redmond."

"That must've been a long time ago," I replied. "I don't recall what the method was."

"In the midst of all the noise and the firing of blank cartridges to re-enact a bank robbery, one gunman was using live ammunition and almost killed his intended victim. We must keep Helen away from that staged fight at Boot Hill."

We saw Helen's car in the parking lot near the Saloon, entered the fenced area after buying our tickets, and began searching for her and Eddie. There were several antique store-fronts, and tourists were wandering in and out of the old-fashioned drug store, doctor's office, and souvenir emporium. As we walked hurriedly from one to the other searching for them, we noticed the gang of "toughs" ready to begin the staged encounter with guns. Tourists began lining up facing the stores, some sitting on wooden benches to watch the fight. Jones and I stood in the shelter of the Saloon porch, still scanning the crowd for the two young people.

Insults were traded, daring shouts exchanged, and the shooting began. Just then Helen and Eddie emerged from one of the stores and headed for the benches opposite us to watch the fracas. Jones, ran out toward the right side of the gunmen shouting, "Helen, this way! Hurry!"

Helen looked up, puzzled, and leaned over to see where Jones' call was coming from. The noise of the men's shouts and the loud reports of the blank shots held everyone's attention. Helen, finally spotting Jones and me at the end of the fight arena, hurried toward us, detecting the urgency in Jones' voice.

At that moment Eddie grabbed Helen's arm and roughly pulled her toward us. As he approached he said, "Someone has live ammunition. I felt a bullet whiz by me!" We stood huddled in the sheltered doorway as the pseudo fight ended with applause from the crowd and the carting away of the "dead" men. As the crowd surged toward us to enter the Saloon, Jones said, "The roof. Someone was on the roof!" and ran around to the back of the building with Eddie following. There we could see the outside wooden stairway leading to the second and third stories and a ladder above that to the roof. Eddie climbed up to check the viewpoint and came back with, "Yes, the gunman could've had a clear shot from behind the chimney to the bench in front of the gunfight."

Jones suggested checking the bench, and found a bullet hole. We reported our find to the show director, and he said he would inform the police. But how could we prove it had been freshly made? How could anyone be charged with a crime when there was no victim? Where was the culprit? We berated ourselves for again missing our chance to arrest Roylott, as there was no doubt in our minds that it was he who had fired that bullet.

Still visibly shaken, but assured that Roylott by now was miles away, we entered the Saloon and tried to watch the can-can girls, toasting Helen with root beer and congratulating her and Eddie for their escape from death.

XVI

The Spidery Man on Highway 56

The Wyatt Earp Motel on the east side of Dodge City was a good choice of lodging because of its proximity to the Pancake House Restaurant, and the Pancake House Restaurant was a good place to hold a decision-making meeting the next morning during breakfast. I sat across from Jones. Helen and Eddie sat facing each other, and anyone with little discernment could tell that here was a couple in love. Helen rested her chin in her hand and stared at Eddie with her blue eyes looking into Eddie's brown ones. She believed that Eddie had saved her life by pulling her away from the bench when Jones had called to her. Eddie, believing that Roylott had fired the shot, was now more than ever wanting to be the complete hero. He was seething with hatred for the villain and eager to track him down.

But we felt hopelessly locked in the same situation as before: no proof of his skulduggery, no license plate number to give to authorities, and no idea what his next move would be. We did have a series of events to relate which could prove interesting to the law.

"There's an even greater complication than we faced before," said Jones. "The Santa Fe Trail divides here, west of Dodge City, and there are two different routes, each equally important, but going several hundred miles apart until they join together again in New Mexico."

"And like the previous traps where Roylott was sure there would be no need for further directions, he has failed to leave any clue as to which way he went," I added.

"Why were there two different routes?" asked Eddie.

"The Mountain Route," explained Helen, "goes more directly west into Colorado and turns south to cross Raton Pass into New Mexico. In the old days that route was favored because of greater safety from Indian attack, but until a rancher built a toll road, the pass was so difficult to cross, it took days to conquer, and the Cimarron Cutoff came to be the choice."

"Is the Cutoff shorter?" asked Eddie.

"Yes, by about two hundred miles, according to what I've read," Helen replied. "But there was a long stretch between rivers, and the lack of water was a real disadvantage also."

"Maybe that's why the railroad used the Mountain Route," I said.

"The Mountain Route also has the most famous stopping place, the trading post in Colorado called Bent's Fort," Helen said. "I remember Roylott talking about that fort."

Jones took out the Park Service map and unfolded it. "I think we'd better split up in order to cover both branches of the Trail," she said.

"Helen and I can go out on the Mountain Route," Eddie said.

Jones objected. "I think Helen should ride in our car. Roylott would recognize Helen's car, and she'll be safer with Watling and me."

The discussion went on and the risks calculated from different angles until it was finally decided that Eddie would take Helen's car and start out on the Mountain Route while Jones and I would take Helen with us on the Cimarron Route. The next question was how to keep in touch. The cell phone idea was negated because there were too many "dead spots" in the isolated areas we'd be traveling through. "Remember when we went into the Colorado forest on the Case of the Alien Landing, Watling? Those phones did not work up there at all."

Looking at the map again we decided the next cities of a size big enough to have a motel would be Garden City on the Mountain Route and Elkhart on the

Cimarron. On the map those towns looked large enough to at least have a library or museum and we could leave messages for each other. We checked out of the motel. Jones and I looked away discreetly as Eddie and Helen stood in a protracted goodbye embrace. A September rain emphasized the gloomy mood of parting as we drove away.

As Jones drove, I was supposed to be not only navigating, but also looking for Roylott's black pickup. But Helen and I both began to doze off and, half asleep, I thought I was on an alien planet when I saw an immense field of windmills. It was a forest of tall towers, each with a single gigantic blade turning slowly. It was a wind farm that covered several acres. Then came a series of small towns, each featuring the tall towers of grain elevators beside the highway, looking like castles of the plains. I must have dozed off again because I heard Jones call out, "Watling! Look! A black pickup!" I roused and realized we must have left the main road and were now in a more hilly area. Off to the north was a grove of trees next to an arroyo and the rear of a vehicle protruded from a clump of bushes there.

"This time we'll get a license plate number," I said, as Jones brought the car to a stop at the edge of the road. She began running toward the black truck, and I followed fumbling with my purse to get pen and writing pad. Helen was climbing out of the back seat saying, "What's up?"

As Jones approached the trees, I could see a tall spidery-looking man dressed in brown, seemingly all arms and legs, coming out of the arroyo. He was emerging from a big conduit, the pipe which ran under the road. It was a circular metal tube big enough to house a large green truck which was parked there. At the same time, I was coming close enough to see that the black pickup in the bushes had a rusted metal fender on the near side and cracked glass in the window. It was not Roylott's.

The spidery man shouted something to Jones, then ran forward and grabbed her. The struggle lasted only an instant. Then the spidery man was on the ground, and Jones was running back toward the car. He was pursuing her, but I was in the car and had it started when she and Helen jumped in and we sped away.

"Guy's crazy," panted Jones. "Drugs. There's something illegal going on there for sure."

"You did great! That was a quick pushover," I said. "You proved that it helps to be in shape for a quick sprint."

"I kneed him as soon as I had space," Jones replied. "The pickup wasn't Roylott's, but I assume you got the number?"

"She got it," Helen said. "So we have a number to report to the police, even though it's not the one we wanted."

XVII

The Encounter at Elkhart

That adventure kept us well awake for the rest of the afternoon, and we continued west, staying on Highway 56. At Elkhart, on the border of Oklahoma, we found the Elkhart Motel and were happy to see a VACANCY sign in front. Inside the office we rang a bell to call the owner and while we waited, studied the huge wire cage in the corner. It looked large enough to hold a gorilla. Then we heard rattling and clicking and the grinding of gears as a little elevator appeared descending within in the wire cage. Out stepped Charlene, the owner, who greeted us warmly. "You're lucky to get a room," she said. "The bird hunters and the construction men have taken most of them. The elevator? Oh yes, my husband installed that for me. It certainly saves running up and down stairs. Messages for Jones, Watling, or Stoner? No, I haven't received any calls for those names. You're traveling the Trail? Well, this is the best place to walk on it because there's a path right along the original Trail here. It's on the National Grasslands, so you don't have to climb fences or get permission from ranchers."

When we told her we were driving rather than hiking, she explained that we could drive on a road through the grasslands that would take us to the spring and the Point of Rocks. "Very much worth seeing," she said. We called the motels in Garden City, but no Eddie Robledo had checked in or had left any messages. It was a worrisome evening in spite of our anticipation for seeing the Grasslands.

So our main goal in the morning was to try to make contact with Eddie by calling the library or museum in Garden City. Thinking he may have used the same idea, we decided to visit the Morton County Museum in Elkhart first. But the car would not start. Jones opened the hood and told us that if we stood there staring into the engine, advice would come.

She was right. As the hunters and construction men came out of the motel rooms to load their cars, they gathered around asking about the problem. Soon there were six or eight, all offering different opinions:

Do you have enough gas?
Probably the battery. I've got jumper cables to get

you started.
It's probably the alternator. Getting it started
wouldn't cure the problem.
Did the engine turn over at all? Could be a
clogged fuel line.
Or the fuel pump.
Probably the computer.

Then a burly gentleman with white sidewhiskers intruded with a solution. "If all of us lend a hand, we can push the car across the street to Kindly Motors. They can check to see what's wrong."

And they did. The Kindly Motors owner said, "Sure we'll check it out. My crew isn't here yet, but let me give you a ride to the museum. I'll call you there when we locate the problem."

The burly gentleman broke in with, "I'm headed out north and can give you a ride to the museum. It's on the main road not far from here. You're Trail buffs? There's a good place there to walk the Trail. And the museum has a great Santa Fe Trail section. Buffalo, wagon, a big mural, artifacts. I wrote one of the brochures you'll see in the book corner."

We introduced ourselves and learned he was Joe Gregg, rancher to the north of Elkhart. As we rode he continued, "I'm a member of the SFTA also. The Cimarron Cutoff Chapter over in Clayton, New Mexico, is planning a wagon train ride down the Trail.

Boy Scouts and Girl Scouts will be learning what it was like to go across the prairie in the old days."

"That sounds like fun," said Helen. "Will they travel on the road or go on the original trail?"

"On the actual Trail. New Mexico has the largest stretch of original trail ruts. Of course, the advance planning required is a big headache: getting permission of land owners for crossing their land and opening fences, insurance liability, environmental protection, and so forth. But it'll all come together pretty soon. We're even bringing mules for some of the wagons. It'll be the real thing."

We arrived at the museum and thanked him, promising to pick up his brochure. Inside, we asked about Eddie and if we could contact the museum or library in Garden City. Still no results. The museum was one of the largest we had visited and the Santa Fe Trail section was truly impressive. The docent led us toward that hall but stopped to turn on the lights, resulting in my being the first to enter the room. Just before the lights came up, I saw a woman in a bonnet and dark dress standing beside a covered wagon. When the room was fully lighted, the figure had disappeared.

Entering the room was like stepping out onto the actual Trail because there was a high ceiling and extensive wall space painted to resemble the grassy plain with buffalo grazing there. In the distance a caravan of covered wagons came toward us. The reality of the impression was enhanced by a mounted buffalo standing in front of the mural looking as if it had just stepped out of the scene, and the actual covered wagon looked as if it were part of the painted caravan. We studied the time line on a far wall, looked at the artifacts, and admired the animal replicas, especially the coyote, prairie dog, and rattlesnake near the wagon.

As we left I purposely lingered, waiting for the docent to douse the lights again, so I could see if the shadow of the woman would reappear. But as I reached the door and turned to look, even before the lights went dim, the figure reappeared! It was Lucille. Her face was shadowed by the big bonnet, but she was facing me and pointing downward as if trying to call my attention to something under the wagon.

I was terribly shaken and unable to say anything as we left the Santa Fe Trail Hall. Jones and Helen were praising the exhibits when I heard Helen ask, "Did you see the pioneer woman near the wagon?"

"No," Jones answered. "Was she a part of the mural?"

"She was pointing down at the snake, I think," Helen replied.

I was relieved to know that the ghost was not my exclusive vision and that I no longer needed to question my own sanity regarding hallucinations. But I was reluctant to confide in Helen, and the incident left me with a strange feeling of foreboding.

XVIII

Lost on the Trail

At the museum lobby desk we found that Kindly Motors had called with the message that the problem with the car was a defective alternator and that a replacement part had to be ordered from Amarillo. The car would not be ready before the next day. We stood in the lobby debating our next move and expressing our concern regarding Eddie.

"I'll call the police. We can't report him as a missing person until after twenty-four hours, but they can be on the lookout," Jones said. "And as long as we're here for another day, we have to make the best of it. And look, here's the book we've been wanting: *Following the Santa Fe Trail: A Guide for Modern Travelers*, by Simmons and Jackson.

I said, "Marc Simmons? Oh, yes, that's the name of the man we met on Pawnee Rock, the one who read to us out of that diary. What a find! Too bad we didn't get his autograph in this book. Well, now we can read our Trail books we've been acquiring. Or we can get some exercise by walking part of the Trail on the Grasslands. How far is it from here?"

As we continued discussing our next moves, a young woman wearing a Forest Service uniform came in and said, "Hi. I'm Sally, the new clerk at the Cimarron Grasslands office. I'm here distributing our new brochure. Have you been out to our office? It's just up the road from here."

After we explained our situation, she said, "I've got a great offer for you. I'm headed north onto the Grasslands area and can take you to the Conestoga Trailhead. From there you can follow the path back along the Trail for three miles—just a nice hike before the heat of the day. You'll come out on the main road again, and I can pick you up in an hour or so."

We liked her suggestion, and in her car she explained further. "There's a limestone post every little way, so even if you go off the path, you can find your way back. The Trailheads are named for the old wagon makers. I'm letting you out at Conestoga. At the southwest end of the Grasslands is the Murphy Trailhead."

The Conestoga Trailhead, neatly fenced, featured a D.A.R. marker, a Grasslands sign, privies, and a long handled pump. "The heat of the day, as far as I'm concerned," said Helen, "is with us already. Can some-body pump while I put my head under the water?"

I complied with alacrity, and Jones followed, so that we all started with cool heads. Outside the fence we saw a double-track path heading away toward the west. I started following it until Jones called, "That's not the Trail. Remember the original Trail is just a set of overgrown ruts, and Sally told us the mowed walking path would parallel it. This looks like a ranch lane or an old road."

So we searched outside the fenced area, not finding a mowed path, but spotting a limestone post, one of the designated markers. On reaching it however, we saw no path or any other signs, so we cut back to the two-tracked lane I'd first seen and followed it. It seemed to go in a westerly direction, but over a couple of hills, it ended at an oil-well pump.

We turned south trying to find the path again and did find another limestone post that had been knocked over and was now hidden in the grass. "Probably knocked over by the cows," explained Jones. "But I think Sally was mistaken in believing this section of the path has been mowed."

We spread out and walked in what was a southwest-erly direction, trying to find more posts or other markers. Our progress was hampered by the heat because our wet-head remedy quickly evaporated. Tiny 'stick-tights,' prickers scratched our ankles and stuck onto our pants legs and socks.

"Can't we find an easier way than this?" I complained. "I think we're wandering and will miss the road by going in circles." I had started with the exhilaration of being in the open under a huge sky and admiring the beauty of the rolling prairie land. Now I was concerned that we were lost and that Sally would be worried as she waited for us long-overdue hikers.

"Even if we're not on the path," Jones stated, "we know the Trail goes generally southwest in this area, and my little watch-band compass shows that we are going southwest." Helen and I followed her doggedly, but wondered why "southwest" always coincided with the worst patches of stickers and yucca. Then Helen yelled, "Snake!" She ran back toward me and said, "Don't go that way. I heard him buzz. I know it's a rattler."

Finally we came to a windmill next to a water tank. We dipped our arms and faces into it, took off our shirts and soaked them also, grateful to feel cool for a few more minutes. Then Jones climbed up onto the braces of the windmill support to the ladder, and from there halfway to the top, using it as a spotting tower she called down to us, "We're headed right. I can see the road from here."

But again her southwest sight-line route led us down and up out of three or four deep arroyos before we arrived, red-faced and exhausted, at the road. Our "one-hour hike" had turned into more than three! Just then we saw Sally's vehicle approaching. "I'm sorry to be so late. I must apologize for making you wait in this heat," she said.

"Oh, we weren't waiting," said Helen. "We were well occupied interacting with Mother Nature and the Santa Fe Trail."

Sally took us back to our motel where we found two pieces of good news: the car would be ready by afternoon of the next day, and best of all, there was a message from Eddie. Charlene had written it down for us and we read

Found Roylott. Am within listening distance. Continue west. Boise City News will have my next message in three days, Eddie

We were happy, but a little confused. What did he mean "listening distance"? As to the Boise City News, Charlene said that was an Oklahoma newspaper in that town, again close to the Trail. Evidently Eddie was able to spy on Roylott and would learn his plans. We relaxed, freed from the heat of the afternoon and from the worry about Eddie. We found a recommended restaurant, and as we ate our steak dinner, we made plans for the morrow—a drive along the rest of the Grasslands Trail to Point of Rocks and then to follow the Trail into Oklahoma.

Mr. Kindly of Kindly Motors insisted we take a loaner car until ours was repaired, so we started out, this time with a picnic, to follow the Grasslands Trail. We found the mowed path down the Trail from our previous hike. We stopped the car several times to walk on the path, admiring the white thistle flowers and the tall grass in an area that had been restored and re-planted with native grass to give back the original landscape when the buffalo had roamed there. We understood better the comparison of the prairie to a Sea of Grass and why the covered wagons were designated Prairie Schooners. We ate our picnic lunch in the Grassland Park.

Driving on to Middle Spring, we walked around in its shady grove along the stream, then went on to Point of Rocks, the famous landmark on the Trail, a high promontory from which we could see along a great stretch of the valley. We admired the yellow leaves of the cottonwood trees on the banks of the river, making the scene a golden wonderland. When the Grassland road and path ended at Murphy Trailhead, we were near the Colorado border. We wanted to continue, but the fence was marked private land and trespassing was prohibited.

As I drove back to Elkhart, Jones read aloud the information regarding the Murphy wagons. "In the early trading days, wagons from the U.S. were stopped at the border of what was then Mexico and required to pay a five-hundred dollar duty for each wagonload of goods crossing the border. The savvy traders soon got the idea to bring bigger wagons and unload several smaller wagons, packing the goods into one large one. The

Murphy Wagon, manufactured by Joseph Murphy in St. Louis, had wheels seven feet high. A man standing inside could barely see over the edge of the wagon bed. The tongue was fifty feet long and the wagon was drawn by four pairs of oxen.

Charlene made some phone calls for us that evening, getting permission from one of the Colorado ranchers to hike along a little stretch of the Trail on his property, so the next morning we drove, this time in Helen's repaired car, quite a distance north, then west into Colorado, and after following twisty ranch roads, came to the T-Bar ranch. Mr. Barr said it was pretty windy for hiking, but he could take us out to the D.A.R. marker in the middle of a pasture and we could hike back to the ranch house from there.

He let us out near the marker which looked similar to all the other D.A.R. markers, except this one had been encircled with a huge tractor tire for protection. We agreed regarding the wind. In fact, it was so strong we felt as if the one mile walk was actually five in effort. We leaned against the wind and lost our footing between gusts. We had brought along sack lunches for picnicking on the Trail, but decided to take them down into the shelter of the river bottom among the trees in order to eat. The day gave us another insight into what the early traders on the Trail must have encountered and gave us a new appreciation of their difficulties.

XIX

Dinner at Black Mesa, Oklahoma

We checked out of the Elkhart Motel the next morning, said goodbye to Charlene, and crossed into Oklahoma. The Trail goes across what is called the Panhandle of Oklahoma, an area once known as "No-Man's Land." We checked in our growing collection of brochures and books to see why it had that designation. We learned that when Kansas became a territory in 1854, its boundary was at the 37th parallel. Texas had no sovereignty north of 36 degrees and 30 minutes, leaving a strip of land 34 miles wide and 168 miles long between Kansas and Texas with no status, no laws, and no law enforcement for the settlers there. It became a haven for bandits and rustlers who would demand "ransom" from cattle drovers bringing herds north into

Kansas. Settlers petitioned Congress to be recognized as Cimarron Territory, but the land was finally attached to Oklahoma in 1890 as Beaver County.

We also read about the caravan caught in 1844 in a late fall blizzard with mules that were already weakened from hunger. About one hundred of the animals huddled together and died in the storm. The wolves and coyotes cleaned the bones by summer, and caravans that came along later would rearrange the skulls and bones into circular or fanciful designs when they stopped to camp there.

We stopped at the museum in Boise City, Oklahoma, and got permission and directions to Autograph Rock, a place on private property where the travelers of early days had camped and carved their names on the sandstone cliff. Although there was no positive indication we'd find a message from Roylott there, it was a possibility. And Helen wanted to see it. "My stepfather has talked about that place so much. Photos would add to my research."

So we postponed getting back to the newspaper office and took the side trip to Autograph Rock. We marveled at the calligraphy and artistry of some of the signatures, done with the precision of tombstone markers. It was in a pleasant grove alongside a creek that tempted us to linger longer, but we were eager to see if there was a message from Eddie.

Kathy Richardson, the pretty lady who managed the Boise City News office, welcomed us and told us we had an e-mail message:

*Found a mtg of the SFTA at Ulysses and followed
the group to Wagon Bed Spring. Man named Jeff
Trotman took us there. Spring and river all dry,
but interesting tour. Next to Bent's Fort, a great
place, restored to original. Attended another mtg.
of SFTA there. Met Roylott. He doesn't suspect my
connection. Wondered about the New Mexico
license plate on the car. He has a pit bull dog. Also
interested in snakes. I'm sticking close to learn his
next plan. Headed for McNees Crossing in New
Mexico I think. Leave message w/ your next location for me at Boise City. Eddie*

Kathy recommended a bed-and-breakfast ranch near
the little town of Kenton, Oklahoma, about an hour
away. It was Black Mesa B&B. She said they have
computer access, several rooms, and are close to Trail
sites. We phoned and found they had vacancies, left the
address with Kathy and drove west to find it.

The flat open plains gave way to rolling hills with
colorful rock formations. The B&B was located at the
base of the huge Black Mesa, known as the highest point
in Oklahoma, almost 5,000 feet high. Owners Vicki and
Monty Joe Roberts welcomed us warmly and showed
us up an outside winding staircase to the spacious loft
containing several beds. Vicki was a comely barefooted
Amazon; Monty Joe, a tall gentleman with a Salvador
Dali mustache. Vicki asked if we'd had supper and when

we told her we planned to go to the local restaurant, she said, "I'm afraid there's no local restaurant under an hour away. But you're welcome to join our party at my sister's house. It's the next ranch back toward Boise City and there's plenty of food because it's potluck and everyone always brings double."

We accepted and found ouselves guests at one of the most entertaining parties I've ever attended. The family party included about thirty people plus children and dogs; and after a supper which featured all kinds of casseroles, salads and cakes, we sat around a huge kitchen table talking over the latest news from each of the families, the weather, and the current price of beef. When Sam, the host, learned that we were following the Santa Fe Trail, he asked, "Did you go out in that wind, the other day? It like to blew my truck off the road coming back from Clayton."

An older bearded gentleman put in, "Good day for a wind wagon. Course, you've heard about Windwagon Thomas on the Trail? My grampa used to tell about him. Heard it from his grampa, I guess."

We said we hadn't, and as the coffee came around for refills, it didn't take much urging for him to tell us about it.

"Seems this feller who used to be a sailor got the idea that with so much wind across the prairie, a wagon could be rigged with sails instead of hitched to mules. He even applied for a patent for the kind of wheels and steering

146

he designed. At first he had a hard time convincing investors to finance the company. He rigged up a kind of prototype and ran it clear to Council Grove from Westport. Got the signature of a blacksmith there, a guy that everyone knew, which proved that he'd gotten there all right. So the men who'd made fun of him before, actually formed a company, the Overland Navigation Company, and put up money to have a big wind wagon made. I guess it looked like a regular wagon, except larger with a big mast, and the tongue of the wagon became the tiller. So you might say the thing went backwards. Well, anyway the day came to test 'er out. They got oxen to haul it out of town, then put up the big sail. Most of the investors were on board for the ride except one doctor who rode along behind on his mule. He said he'd be the one to keep pace and estimate the speed of the thing, but some people said, knowing all the dangers, he'd brought along his doctor bag with plenty of bandages and liniment. Anyway they got 'er rigged and started out. The wind was plenty strong that day and the boat started out at a good clip. Doctor could hardly keep up even though his mule was supposed to be one of the fastest animals around.

It went so fast the men inside began to have doubts that they wanted to stay aboard. Old Windwagon Thomas was up front behind the mast, shouting 'Watch me bring 'er around!' But then something happened. The steering gear locked up and the thing kept turning till it was going backward in a big circle. The men started jumping off and running to get out of the way of the next pass. Windwagon, he didn't even realize he was losing his crew until the whole boat crashed up against a fence. And that was the end of that company."

Some of the listeners laughed; others expressed doubt of the validity of the story. But the bearded gentleman insisted, "Swear to God it's true. You can look it up."

When we asked if that was the end of Windwagon Thomas, he continued, "Some say he went on to the next town and built more sail wagons, actually took freight clear to Santa Fe. Indians used to talk about seeing a big white tepee sailing over the hills. But all that was just before the railroads started, and I guess the trains became more of a sure thing for hauling the goods."

"Wish that wind would bring a little more rain with it. The Cimarron is so low it's drying up in spots along my place." The speaker was a man in a green flannel shirt with yellow neckerchief. "Reminds me of the guys that first came along the Jornada. I'm glad we don't have it that bad."

The speaker's son, a mischievous looking imp, probably prompted to give his cue, asked, "How bad was it?" and his father began, "This was one of the first groups to travel the Santa Fe Trail. Bill Becknell was the leader and thought they'd save time going more directly south from the Arkansas River to reach Santa Fe. But they ran out of water before reaching the

Cimarron. They got so thirsty and desperate they killed the dogs and cut the ears off the mules to drink the blood. They didn't realize they were getting near to the Cimarron and almost decided to try to go back to the Arkansas. Then they saw a buffalo, killed it and found its stomach full of water. They drank that filthy stuff and got enough strength to go on toward the river. Then filled their canteens and came back to rescue the others. They finally made it, but from then on everyone was warned about the distance across the Jornada."

"Is that really true?" inquired a little girl who sat near me.

"Sure is. You can look it up," the storyteller replied.

"Where were the moms?" the little girl asked. "They would know to take enough water along."

After the laughter subsided, the storyteller explained. "The Trail was mostly a trading trail for selling goods in Santa Fe or Mexico. Not very many families came along until later in the century. So it was mostly all men. The trip was considered too rough for women."

"What about Susan Magoffin?" Vicki asked. "She went down the Trail with her husband all the way into Mexico."

"Well, she rode in comfort and style," the storyteller answered. "Her husband led the expedition, she rode in a carriage instead of a wagon, and they set up a fancy tent for her every night."

"But you remember," Vicki countered, "She was pregnant at the time. Her buggy was upset when they crossed a creek, and her injury caused her to have a miscarriage. You can look it up!"

The laughter died down and everyone agreed that both men and women had it a lot rougher in the old days on the Trail. One man said he believed the worst thing would be seeing those mirages of lakes of water when they were so thirsty. The talk about mirages led to experiences with visions and from thence to ghost stories. I thought about Lucille, but I was not brave enough to tell about her. Who would believe that a Scottish lady of long ago in Westport was following a middle-aged secretary in modern days down the Santa Fe Trail to scare her? Or was it to warn her? I did not know it then, but I found out later that it proved to be the latter.

The next morning at a breakfast of pancakes, eggs, bacon, and several kinds of home-made jellies, we talked with the other guests around the big table. Mr. and Mrs. Allen were members of the High Point Society and were planning to climb Black Mesa. The High Pointers had the goal of climbing the highest point in each state of the U.S., and the B&B frequently hosted guests who were aiming to conquer Black Mesa because it was officially the highest point in Oklahoma.

Vicki was called to the phone with an inquiry about reservations for the weekend. She returned to the table laughing at the questions the caller had asked. "He wanted to know how far to the nearest post office," she said. "And how far it was to a department store." She had to explain that the charm of this B&B was its very rural setting, quite far away from cities of any size. We had fun speculating on the kind of tourist he might be.

"Maybe he thinks he'll need special western clothes and plans to shop here after he sees what we look like."

"Maybe he wants to carry on his business correspondence, and stay in touch with his broker."

"He probably doesn't know we have a computer, a web site, and e-mail access."

"Maybe he's a fugitive from justice and has his photo on the post office wall."

The last comment elicited some laughter and a prompt by Monty Joe. "Vicki, why don't you sing the song the hiking women taught us." We all seconded his suggestion and Vicki sang:

Mention my name down in Kenton
It's the greatest little town in the world
I used to live there but don't any more
I was Miss Kenton back in nineteen-oh-four

I was a big shot down at the city hall
They've even got my picture on the post office wall

Mention my name down in Kenton
And if you ever get in a jam
Just mention my name
I said mention my name

But please don't tell them where I am!

Applause, laughter, and requests for more coffee, toast, and prickly-pear jelly were followed by discussion of plans for the day. Helen said, "I've been reading in the *Land of Enchantment* book that Eddie bought me about Marian Russell. She went along the Trail so many times. It's really romantic how she met her husband, and went with him to Fort Nichols. Fort Nichols is near here, isn't it? I'd like to see it."

"Actually it was more of a camp than an established fort," Monty Joe said. "It was in operation only a few months. But you can still see the outline of where the walls were and the dents of the dugouts. They lived in tents pitched over depressions in the ground. It's on private ranch land, but we can call the owners and get permission for you to hike to it."

Jones thought the idea a good one, and I commented, "I can see it's happening. We're becoming addicts, real Trail junkies. Even Jones is falling under the spell of the Santa Fe Trail. We were told this would happen."

Of course Helen was delighted with the prospect of adding to the notes for her thesis, but Jones, the realist and anti-romantic, had to conceal her liking with a rational justification, "The more we know about the Trail, the more we can understand the mind of our antagonist and eventually out-smart him."

Her comments gave rise to questions about the

"antagonist," and Jones quickly made up a story to gloss over our travels under the guise of playing a game for a "contest" which was sponsored by the Santa Fe Trail Association. I admired her quick thinking and the smooth extrication from a complicated situation.

Vicki began clearing the table, and Monty Joe went to the office to check his e-mails. Helen went with him to check for any messages for us. She came back shortly with a message.

See you at the Clayton Fandango Saturday night. Eddie

"What is the Clayton Fandango?" we asked. Vicki replied by bringing a brochure from the office which explained. It was the newsletter for the Cimarron Cutoff Chapter of the Santa Fe Trail Association, listing up-coming events, among which was the dance party to be held in the Eklund Hotel in Clayton, New Mexico.

"Fandango was the name of a Spanish dance, but then it meant the celebrations held by the traders along the Trail, and now it's a dance party, any kind of foolishness with music and food," said Monty Joe.

"We won't be able to attend because we have guests that night, but it will be pretty special because the Eklund Hotel has finally finished their refurbishing and will be using the new ballroom for the first time," said Vicki.

"But you know," added Monty Joe, "most fandangos ended in a big brawl. This is rough western country. You may find yourself in the midst of a big fight."

"Oh, shush, Monty Joe," Vicki replied. "Don't try to scare these ladies. D.Ray, the man who organizes the Trail parties, will keep everything very proper. Probably the only disagreement will be between Mrs. Pettigrew and Zeke Boon about whether to have the fancy Regency dances or American squares. I think with D.Ray in charge he will compromise and have both. It will be a nice party."

"Oh, look," said Helen, still perusing the bulletin. "Here's a notice about that covered wagon trip that Mr. Gregg told us about. It's next week. They want more adults to join."

"We'll be fortunate to make it to the fandango. We're not prepared with the proper clothes for a fandango, let alone camping outfits for the Trail," I said. We had not come prepared for more than a weekend, and now our outfits were becoming rather rumpled. "Will everyone be dressed frontier style for the fandango?"

"A long skirt for the women, and the men need only to tuck their pants into their boots and wear a big neckerchief," said Vicki. "There's a clothing store in Clayton that carries fancy duds, but it has a consignment department that sells used clothes and costumes too, if you need to shop for something. But you'll enjoy the party no matter what you wear."

We agreed it sounded like fun, and as we had tomorrow to get there, decided to visit Camp Nichols today. The Allens left to hike up Black Mesa, and we followed the map Monty Joe had drawn for us to drive to the Steele Ranch.

It was another hot day, and we feared for the car as we drove down a rather bumpy lane. One big swing gate opened and closed easily, but the next one was difficult to open, so we left the car, climbed through the barbed wire, and began hiking in the direction indicated on the map.

Rolling pasture land did not allow a distant view and the cow paths all looked similar, criss-crossing, going into and out of gullies. Finally, Jones spied a flag pole in the distance and we altered our course to walk toward it. It was the camp. Had it not been for the flag pole, we'd have gone past it, because from the stream bed the little mesa appeared as just another hill. But when we arrived on top we could see rocks, and brush with depressions in the ground and low signs indicating where the various parts of the camp had been.

"Look! Here it is," called Helen. "The Russells had their tent right here."

"And here is Kit Carson's name," I added.

"This is the real thing, all right," Jones said. "Look over there. Real buffalo in that next field." We wandered the area looking at the boundaries of the hospital, the kitchen, and the headquarters, before sitting down near the Russell dugout to eat our sack lunches.

The return walk was more direct, and back at the B&B we had fun exchanging the tales of our experiences with the Allens. Mrs. Allen was not as enthusiastic as her husband. "It took us all morning to get up there," she said. "And at the top, you can't imagine how big and flat the top of it is. We took pictures of each other at the obelisk, so we'll have proof that we got to Oklahoma's high point."

"The best part was the view from on top," Mr. Allen said. "We could see into Colorado and New Mexico. This really is a three-state corner."

"I can take you to see the dinosaur footprints tomorrow," Vicki offered. But we declined in favor of starting out for Clayton in order to shop for frontier outfits for the fandango. Our exhausted state due to the long hike was partly remedied by the supper of roast beef, tossed salad, black-eyed peas, corn bread and chocolate cake. Later we tried to watch a Trail video in our loft bedroom, but fell asleep before it ended.

A barking dog wakened me in the night, and when I turned over in bed, I saw the dark figure of Helen seated on the side of her cot and staring out the window. I knew she was worrying about Eddie and the danger from Roylott.

And then one of those demons of the wee hours invaded my own imagination. What if Eddie and Roylott were in cahoots! How could this be? Even though Eddie had watched Roylott set up the falling-stone trap at

Hermit's Cave, had he been able to identify him in the dim morning light? And even if he had found Roylott on the Mountain Route, was Eddie immune to bribery? He looked as if he admired Helen, but his threadbare clothes indicated poverty, and his naivete and personable friendliness could make him vulnerable. And Roylott's skill at dissembling, his friendliness to young people, his clever machinations and contacts in the Trail Association, all left room in my mind for this terrible idea. There was no proof that it was Roylott who had set all the traps. Could the spidery man be in his employ?

My demon worries circulated and re-circulated, keeping me awake long after Helen had fallen asleep, and the effects of my insomnia were visible the next morning because Jones asked, "Did you sleep well, Watling? You look a little gray around the gills."

"Maybe too much chocolate cake last night," I replied.

XX

A Fracas at the Clayton Fandango

After another bountiful breakfast we left the Black Mesa B&B, and just after the village of Kenton, crossed the state line into New Mexico.

Vicki and Monty Joe told us we'd pass another famous Trail site on the way, McNee's Crossing. He told us that McNees and Munro, two scouts riding ahead of their wagon train, had stopped to rest there. While taking their siesta, they were attacked and shot with their own guns. When the wagon train came upon the scene, McNees was dead and Munro was dying. A band of Indians rode up, probably innocent of any knowledge of what had happened, but because the traders in the caravan assumed they were the culprits, fired on them. That classic encounter was the cause of renewed hostilites between the traders and the Indians.

When we came upon the sign next to the road, it was not enough to photograph the sign. We had to visit the actual site. So we opened a gate and drove part way toward the river. When we arrived at a windmill and water tank, we were approached by a herd of cows. Helen and I were a little nervous. "I hope there aren't any bulls planning to charge us."

Jones pooh-poohed our concern. "These are just moms, steers, and calves. They're coming toward us because they're expecting we have something for them to eat. In the winter the rancher comes out with bales of hay for them."

The cattle stopped a few yards away and looked at us curiously. A small white obelisk nearby attracted our attention. Helen read it aloud, all the while looking nervously toward the cows. The message showed that the site commemorated a special celebration.

Here on the morning of July 4th, 1831, the day was appropriately celebrated by citizens of the United States, members of a freight caravan from Independence, Mo, to Santa Fe, recorded by Josiah Gregg, member of the party. This is the first authentic observance on present Union County soil, the Territory then being a part of the Republic of Mexico.

The marker included names of the American Legion

members who had erected the marker in 1921. We walked down to the river, noting the shelf-like rock shore, the shallow water, and the indention on the banks showing where the wagons had crossed. There were no trees, and very little vegetation along the shore, but the stark landscape carried the aura of a dramatic past.

As we drove toward Clayton, we noticed some distant mountains on the western horizon. "The guide book says we're seeing Rabbit Ears mountain, but it doesn't look much like a rabbit's ears to me," I said. We drove on into Clayton, a town that had kept its storm ditches as paved dips crossing the main street. They were effective speed bumps. It was easy to find the clothing store on the main street also, and we were amazed at the style and elegance of the collection. Helen found a blue velvet and satin ensemble with full skirt and fitted bodice that complemented her blue eyes. Jones and I asked to see the less expensive costumes in the consignment department. A black dress with long sleeves was Jones' choice, but being a bit plumper and a good deal shorter, I was not as easy to fit. Finally, a lacy long-sleeved white blouse, and a brown full skirt, that miraculously did not need altering, fitted the bill, and we felt ready to fling ourselves into the fandango. There were no vacancies at the Eklund, but we found rooms at a nearby motel and proceeded to primp ourselves into what we thought would be the proper 19th century western style.

The Eklund Hotel stood on a main corner in Clayton. The Trail and community organizations had helped to maintain its historical integrity, and the three-story building with portico and second floor balcony was newly painted and restored to grand Victorian style. We climbed a curving staircase to the second-floor ballroom and were delighted with its size, the smooth floor, and the decor with lighted lanterns on little tables around the entire room. A fire in a huge brick and marble fireplace at the far end of the hall added a welcome warmth.

We were greeted by D.Ray, the host, a tall man of splendid manners and precise speech. His costume of white shirt and silk cravat, striped blue pants and soft boots was a compromise between Victorian elegance and the western American frontier. He bowed and expressed gratitude that we had arrived early because the program began with instructions in English contra dancing and two more couples were needed. Jones graciously offered to dance the man's part to a waiting elderly lady in a pink dress, and D.Ray lined us up for the first figure. A trio of piano, violin, and drum furnished some tinny but rhythmic music, and we began with a dance called Sir Roger de Coverly. It resembled the familiar Virginia Reel and the dancers quickly picked up the proper sequence of steps.

But after repeating the routine we were mainly concerned with watching the doorway for Eddie. Realizing that we had arrived early, we did not worry so much at first, but as the dances followed one after the other, and became increasingly complicated, I could see that Helen was losing interest in the dance. The long lines of dancers, men on one side and ladies on the other, faced each other, moved together and apart, circled, weaved in and out, casted up or down, and repeated a sequence with the couples taking turns in the movements which led each couple toward the head of the hall. The piano player sang

My bonny belle
You know me well
Kiss me quick
I'll never tell

The first of May
We'll well away
And where we'll go
I cannot say

Jones had noticed that the piano was a double mechanical; that is, it operated by pumping the pedals to play the perforated rolls, but could also furnish music as a regular pianoforte with a pianist. When the set ended and she was no longer needed to even up the genders, she offered to pump the instrument with some of the contra dance rolls of music that were stored in the piano bench. She went at it energetically and enjoyed herself as much as the dancers who continued gliding to the tinny music.

Suddenly we became aware of additional people coming into the hall, mostly men in heavy boots and big western hats. Laughing and stomping, they entered the room and changed the party completely. A fat man with goatee and red suspenders approached the piano and unceremoniously took over. "Slide over, Babe," he said to Jones. "It's my turn to tickle these ivories." Jones frowned at his discourtesy but graciously stood up and left the piano. He began thumping out a polka and singing

My wife and I live all alone
In a little ole hut we call our own
She loves gin and I love rum
I tell you what we do have fun
Ah ha ha, you and me
Little brown jug how I love thee!

The violin player fiddled along as if he'd been waiting for the chance to speed up the tempo, and the drummer thumped along, loudly emphasizing his approval. The men who had just entered grabbed the ladies away from their partners and began spinning them around the room. A few women backed away and refused to dance, but the majority went along happily with the changed program. Before realizing it, I too was swept into the throng, by none other than Mr. Gregg, the burly rancher from Elkhart. As we gyrated around the room, we passed Helen with her new partner who turned out to be Eddie himself. Both were smiling happily as they whirled by. Even Jones had been forced into the fray by a wiry little man in green coveralls, a foot shorter than she, who jumped vertically at each step. They made a comic pair indeed.

D.Ray was not happy. "These ruffians don't even remove their hats in a ballroom," he said. " Now the square dancing will begin, and I hope the new floor will hold up under all the stomping."

As the tune ended, an angular slouching man with glasses and straw hat stepped up to the piano and gave orders. "Don't set down. Keep your partner. Square your sets. Catch up and move 'em out!" Most of the original contra dancers found a partner and followed his orders. The piano player thumped and the caller sang.

Allemande left with your left hand
Right to your partner and right and left grand
Corn's in the crib and wheat's in the stack
Meet your partner and turn right back.
I left my gal in Franklin, headin' for Santa Fe
Dancin' with senoritas all along the way

Another square dance followed, and when the pace changed with a waltz, Jones and I left our partners and eagerly caught up with Helen and Eddie to hear the report of his recent activities. Our greatest concern was the whereabouts of Roylott and knowledge of his plans. "He's helping organize the Trail ride across the plains to New Mexico Rock Peak," Eddie said. "He doesn't know Jones and Watling are following the Trail too or that we are in cahoots. He knows Helen is still following the Cimarron Cutoff, and he asked me to be sure she goes on the Trail ride. He almost planned to come to this party tonight, but he had to go to Boise City to make arrangements for another wagon and team. It's going to be quite a caravan. There'll even be a stage coach. But you'll be safe with me, Helen. He may be planning a wagon upset or something, but I'm thinking we can be among the walkers and can watch to stay away from danger."

"Won't most people be riding in the wagons?" Helen asked.

"There are lots of kids and more people than wagons to accommodate them, and the scoutmasters say if we're authentic Santa Fe traders, we'd all be walking because in Trail days the wagons were all filled with goods to sell in Santa Fe. No room to ride."

"Well, are you ready for more hiking, Watling?" Jones asked.

"Maybe I can stand one day in the hot sun," I replied. "But not much more. How long will this thing take?"

"It's scheduled for four days," Eddie explained. "I

don't think we'll be moving that whole time, though. The leaders want to schedule it like the real caravans, stopping to 'noon it' and let the horses graze."

"But the original traders tried to do about ten miles a day, at least," Jones said.

"Oh lordy no! I'll never do it," I was thinking. I wondered if I asked, if I could ride in a wagon. I'd rather chance being upset rather than go limping along through cactus all day long. But not wanting Jones and the young peope to brand me as a wimp, I said nothing.

"There's got to be room for some people to ride." Eddie said. "We'll have food and bed rolls to carry in the wagons, but we're not taking tons of stuff to sell in Santa Fe the way the original traders did."

Our conversation was interrupted with the call to square up for another dance, and the merriment resumed. After an hour or so, D.Ray announced the supper break and we descended to the dining rooms to what was more of a grand banquet than a late supper. The long tables were covered with white cloths and decorated with candles and miniature covered wagons. The food was arranged on a long buffet shelf with such a variety of viands that most of us found our plates were overflowing before we had taken even a sample of each offering. Lemonade was placed on the table in large pitchers, and a coffee urn on a rolling cart kept the diners well supplied, but I noticed that two or three of the late arriving gentlemen produced little flasks and surreptitiously proceeded to strengthen their beverages with liquid of much greater potency.

After such a repast I felt the urge to relax and would have liked to engage in conversation with Mr. Gregg, but we could hear the fiddle being re-tuned, and the young people all climbing back upstairs to resume dancing, so everyone followed to join in. The first two sets of dances went smoothly and were followed by a circle dance which scrambled the arrangement and left everyone with new partners for the waltz which came next. I sat down, glad for the rest, and Jones joined me, glad to be rid of the short leaping man. We refreshed ouselves at the lemonade table and sat near it to watch the dancing.

The room seemed more crowded and warmer from the exertions of the dancers. Windows were opened and the French doors to the balcony folded back. We admired Eddie's finesse in maneuvering during the partner shuffle to regain Helen as his partner, and we admired their smooth turns and graceful steps as they danced together. They seemed a well suited couple. Then a tall thin man in a black western hat, materialized from a corner, tapped Eddie to cut in, and swept Helen away with an awkward shuffle. He vaguely resembled the spidery man of Jones' encounter at the roadside culvert, but I could not be sure. Eddie looked surprised, then disappointed, but politely stood aside till the end of the number. The tall man did not escort

Helen back to a seat, but held her hand and began dancing with her again as the music resumed. Eddie followed them to cut in and regain his partner, but the tall man was manuevering Helen toward the open doors to the balcony. As they reached the doorway and Eddie tapped him, the tall man shouldered him aside. Eddie shouldered back and attempted to pull Helen away, but the tall man pushed harder and releasing Helen's hand, swung a blow at Eddie's head. Eddie ducked and came up with a fist to the tall man's jaw. Helen screamed, and backed away. The tall man stumbled on the edge of the doorway. Eddie grabbed him to turn him for another blow, but he managed to pull Eddie down, and soon the two were on the floor, wrestling and punching. The music stopped, and other men began rushing to see or assist. Instead of attempting to separate the two, the first men also took part in the fracas and the situation threatened to explode into a general brawl.

It was another instance in which Jones' quick thinking and decisive action saved the situation. She ran to the wall switch and turned off the lights. Then grabbing a pitcher of lemonade she proceeded to throw it into the tangled melee, following it with another, until the confused and doused wrangling men turned away from their combatants and tried to attack the douser. But Jones, along with me and several other people, were crowding the stairway to exit the scene. Mr. Gregg and a manager with a booming voice turned on the lights, restored order, and declared the dance party at an end.

We stood on the street in front of the hotel as the excited party goers came out, followed by the disheveled brawlers including Eddie who was bleeding from his nose, and holding his hand against one eye. Helen was with him, crying and trembling and trying to hold her handkerchief to his face. The spidery man was nowhere to be seen.

"I guess Monty Joe was right," I said. "A Santa Fe Trail fandango can be pretty dangerous."

"I think that tall hairy man was going to push me off the balcony," said Helen. "I'm glad he didn't get me out to the railing."

We looked up at the balcony. It was in shadows, lighted only from the hall beyond the French doors.

"Who's that woman looking down at us? Was there a woman at the party wearing a bonnet?" Helen asked.

"I don't think so," said Jones. "Whoever it is probably put it on to come outside."

But I knew it was not any woman who had attended the fandango. The dark figure in the bonnet was Lucille.

XXI

Trail Plans in New Mexico

At the motel Eddie showered the sticky lemonade and the remaining blood off his face and joined us for a debriefing and catch-up. He sat on the floor leaning back against the side of the bed on which Helen sat stroking his hair and touching his bruised face tenderly from time to time.

"Who was that skinny man who was trying to push me off the balcony?" asked Helen.

"He's definitely a goon sent by Roylott," Eddie said.

"Had you seen him before?" Jones asked. "He's definitely an underworld operator." And she went on to relate her encounter with him at the culvert. We sat on the divan which had doubled as a fold-out bed. I removed my shoes and tucked my feet up under me, listening to Jones' account and seconding her impressions of the encounter.

"During the last SFTA meeting at Bent's Fort," said Eddie, "I was sitting by the door and saw that Roylott was called out to talk with someone. I caught a glimpse of his face outside in the patio. I'm sure it was the same guy."

"Well, there's another of Roylott's evil plans gone awry," I said. "But he'll be scheming for the next encounter. I think we'd better stay away from that covered wagon trip."

"I think that Helen should avoid it," said Jones. "But I want to catch him in one of his dirty plots and bring him to justice. I have a plan that I think may work."

"What is it? asked Helen. "I'm sure that with Eddie to protect us and help us, we can finally get him. I want to go with you. Besides, unless he knows I'm on the trip, he won't even try to arrange any dangerous plan."

"We do have the advantage of Roylott's not being aware that we are on the case," I said. "But Helen's safety should be our foremost concern."

The discussion continued with all the facets of the situation being covered, except that Jones could not be convinced to reveal any details of her own plan. She finally conceded that Helen be allowed to go along on the caravan trip, but as they had two days to plan for it, she could incorporate some adjustments to her own scheme and insure Helen's safety at the same time.

Our discussion was interrupted when the phone rang.

The caller was D.Ray apologizing for the fracas and inquiring about Eddie's injuries. He was so solicitous and so desirous of doing something to "amend our impression of the town" that we ended up agreeing to let him escort us through the county museum and out to see the dinosaur prints at Clayton State Park the next day.

Up to this time Jones had not contacted any law enforcement agency, not only because she had insufficient evidence for a criminal charge, but also because she was sure of being able to outwit Roylott and bring him to justice by herself. Now, however, with the knowledge that he and the spidery man were linked in evil, she decided to contact the State Police. So, the next morning, she excused herself from joining us when we met D.Ray at the museum and planned to re-join us at dinner that evening.

The museum tour the next day was fascinating. The building was on three levels and the collection was quite extensive and tastefully displayed. We focused mainly on the Santa Fe Trail section which had numerous artifacts, diaries, and display maps. D.Ray proudly pointed out the newest additions and, wearing white gloves, opened antique trinket boxes and fragile albums for our perusal.

On the ride north of Clayton to the State Park, D.Ray explained that the reason the Rabbit Ear Mountain did not look like rabbit's ears was that it was named, not for the shape of the mountain, but for an Indian chief by that name. He pointed out another mountain named

Mount Clayton, and said that the early travelers and settlers called it Round Mound. It was a main landmark on the Santa Fe Trail and we would be traveling near its base on our caravan trip. "I wish we had time to show you the volcano," D.Ray explained. "Capulin Peak is northwest on the way to Raton. A road spirals around it to the top. Not only do you get a magnificent view, but it's also one of the few extinct volcanos in which you can walk down into the crater."

The park featured a beautiful lake, a picnic pavilion, and several camp sites. But the amazing section was the fossilized dinosaur footprints covering a large area. A viewing platform with explanatory signs kept us fascinated and educated us regarding those prehistoric beasts.

D.Ray had really extended extra time and courtesy to us. At the lunch hour he produced box lunches, especially prepared by the Eklund chef. We sat in the picnic pavilion by the lake and enjoyed the chicken salad, fruit, and spice cake they contained. But in lieu of more touring, we discussed an impending concern, our preparation for the covered wagon trip on the Santa Fe Trail.

"I want some better boots for hiking," said Helen. "Our walk on the grasslands convinced me. No more bare ankles on the Trail."

"Do you have sleeping bags?" D.Ray asked. "And although September is usually dry, you should have rain ponchos, just in case."

"Are air mattresses allowed as part of our baggage?" I inquired. "I dread the thought of sleeping on the ground."

"We'll need sleeping bags," said Eddie. "But let's not bring any extra baggage. I'll bet we'll be tired enough at night to sleep on rocks and not feel them."

I nodded but thought to myself that's an O.K. statement from a twenty-year old, but my middle-aged bones may not agree.

We decided that the rest of the afternoon had better be spent in shopping, so we headed back into Clayton to search for a sports and hunting store that could outfit us properly for the Trail. We checked the motel for a message from Jones, and finding nothing, decided to shop for her, hoping our choices would be agreeable.

When we all met for dinner at the Eklund, she not only approved of our purchases, but also said they fit the requirements of the official caravan leaders, with whom she had been in contact. She laughed at Helen's yellow poncho covered with big black horse-head designs but approved of the sleeping bag and hooded sweatshirt we'd bought for her.

"We're hoping for no rain," I said, "because we're one rain poncho short. I volunteered to be the one without." I was secretly hoping they'd let me ride in a wagon in case of rain.

The Eklund dining room, with its dark paneled walls and antique paintings of western scenes, was reflecting the merriment of a large crowd. We guessed that some of the diners would be our companions on the upcoming Trail trip. Our happy anticipation was sobered by the extra information Jones had acquired. "Mr. Gregg was able to show me the list of travelers and confirmed that Roylott will be with us. He knows Eddie, but I think Watling and I had better wear dark glasses and big hats in order to remain incognito," she said. "Also, after our arrival at Rock Point, we're headed for the end of the Trail in Santa Fe, so I've made reservations there at La Fonda Hotel. It's the official 'Inn at the End of the Trail.'"

"Don't we have to come back here for our cars?" asked Helen.

"We'll go in both cars tomorrow to Rock Point Ranch, leave one car there, and drive back here in the other one for the start of the wagon trek," she explained.

"This gets complicated," I said. "They must have been planning this expedition for a long time. I'm amazed when I think of all those kids, their baggage, the food required, the coordination among the ranchers and Scout leaders, plus the parents who'll be picking the kids up at the end. Wow, it boggles the mind!"

"And that's not the least of it," added Jones. "There is disagreement among the leaders. Some want to allow only animal-drawn wagons, to keep everything as authentic to the original experience of the traders on the Trail as possible, while others, especially those who couldn't hire horses or mules, want to haul a flat-bed trailer with a big John Deere tractor. And there's one rancher who didn't want the procession to cross his land at all. They finally convinced him the numbers would be limited and the damage to his pasture would be minimal. It really is an honor to own a piece of the Trail, and I think it helped to give him an honorary membership in the Santa Fe Trail Association and a promise of honorable mention in the Wagon Tracks newsletter. Mr. Gregg was instrumental in convincing him. Gregg is a diplomatic talker."

"Very personable and nice looking, too," I thought to myself.

Over our flan dessert we finalized our plans for the car shuttle schedule and checked our list for any other items needed for the grand expedition.

XXII

Wagon Train on the Trail

The next morning was clear and cool, and at Jones' insistence, we were up early enough to see the sky go from turquoise to pink to yellow as dawn painted one thin strip of clouds in the east. We checked out of the motel and drove out on the highway, turning off on a road headed south toward the Round Mound mountain. There were already several cars headed in the same direction, and when we arrived at the staging area, we found a crowd assembled waiting for the wagons to arrive. We left our baggage with Helen and Eddie guarding it while we drove to the Rock Point destination.

Had we not been so early, we'd have been able to follow any other car-shuttle travelers, but as it was, we lost our way twice on the little dirt roads angling back toward the

Rock Point Ranch. A short hike up a bumpy driveway to a distant ranch house for inquiry finally put us right, and we spotted the big arched gate and windmill at our destination where we left Helen's car. Driving back to the start in Jones' car, I expressed concern about being so late. "Don't worry," she said. "With all the complications and arrangements, I'll wager it will be late afternoon before we start. I'm glad we brought a snack bag for lunch."

She was right. One of the wagons had not yet come, some cars were still arriving and unloading more youngsters, and the entire scene resembled the setting up of a huge carnival with people going to and fro, animals being led into place, dogs barking, children chasing each other and running to pet the horses and mules. A big stagecoach with four horses was being manuevered into position.

Two of the smaller rigs were attracting most of the attention. Darrell Curbow from Arkansas, besides bringing his own big hand-made wagon and the two Belgian horses, Prince and Charles, to pull it, had just unloaded from a huge semi, a tiny covered wagon and two miniature horses. The children were delighted with the ponies and gathered around to pet them and offer treats. A few parents were taking pictures.

The other tiny covered wagon was actually a golf cart, converted to a covered wagon by the addition of curved metal bows supporting a white canvas. Doug Sofa, the owner, was proudly demonstrating the luggage arrangement and the stash of water, plus extra batteries to power the motor.

We found Joe Gregg, who was one of the designated baggage haulers, and put our gear inside his wagon. Four mules, already harnessed, stood patiently at attention in front.

Farther along the road men were unloading supplies from a truck and stashing them into a chuck wagon. Some men who had parked a boxy white trailer-truck at the head of the line were letting down a stairway from its rear door, and a small line formed to climb the steps. "That's the toilet wagon," Mr. Gregg explained. " We rented it from the movie people in Santa Fe."

A black van labeled KOB-TV turned in off the road, and two men and a woman climbed out and unpacked tripods and black cases of camera equipment. "Well, that ends the 19th century atmosphere," said Jones. "Too bad they can't focus on just the antique wagons and the people in frontier clothes for the television broadcast."

Another big wagon rolled up, pulled by a huge farm tractor. A woman with a clipboard checked her list, ran to Joe Gregg, and announced, "That does it. We're all here." Joe Gregg and the clipboard lady began going among the wagons giving out numbers for the order of march in the caravan lineup. "While we can, we're going to travel in two parallel lines," explained Gregg. "The original caravans went in as many as four lines across here, but we've promised not to trample any more pasture than we need to. Four lines made it easier to circle up for the evening corral and form a defense against possible Indian attack. Also, in case of a break down, the entire line wouldn't be held up."

At the request of the television crew, the four mounted scouts and the authentic-looking wagons with live animals went ahead, accompanied by the Trail buffs who had worn frontier costumes and were walking alongside. Jones, Helen, and Eddie were standing toward the rear of the caravan and I had been talking with Joe Gregg next to his wagon when the signal to start was given. A woman came running up to me with a flowered sunbonnet. "Here! Put this on. You'll be on view in the front." Mr. Gregg graciously offered to have me ride next to him on the driver's bench. I felt relieved to know I didn't have to hoof it, and I accepted the offer with heartfelt thanks. As he helped me up, the traditional cry rang out, "All's set! Spread out! Catch up!" and the caravan began moving slowly past Round Mound. Cries of "Hurrah, Goodbye, and See you next year" filled the air. We were officially underway.

What a thrill! I felt like a fine lady of the frontier as I rode along next to the handsome wagon master, the horsemen ahead and the long train of wagons behind us. As the Trail made a big curve and I could look back, the rear wagons, diminished by distance, looked smaller, and the little pony wagon and golf cart made the distance seem even greater.

"I know there were fewer women than men on the

Trail in the early days," I said. "But I thought there'd be more moms here with so many kids going along."

Gregg laughed. "There are a few Brownie and Cub mothers along, but the older kids always want as few parents along as possible. And most of the older women don't relish the idea of hiking and camping. Those parents that didn't stay home are having a party of their own in Clayton tonight, I hear."

"Is Mrs. Gregg a Trail buff?" I inquired.

"There's no Mrs. Gregg. If there were, she'd have to be a Trail buff for sure." He grinned and flicked his whip above the mules' backs.

"Weren't most of the wagons pulled by oxen in the old days?"

"It depends. Many of the early wagoneers preferred them because, even though they were slower, they were pretty strong, and were not as apt to be stolen by the Indians. A big disadvantage was their feet got sore easily. I've seen some old pictures showing oxen wearing cowhide booties to protect their feet. Course, some took the trouble to have them shod, the way you do a horse, except it was a lot more difficult."

"How so?"

"They have cloven hoofs, requiring two smaller half-moon shaped pieces to be attached to each hoof, and you can't just ask an ox to stand still and lift one leg for shoeing, so they had to be hung up in a giant sling in order to work on their feet."

"That's amazing! On this caravan I see more horses than mules. How did you happen to have mules instead of big horses?"

"Mules are just as strong, maybe stronger for their size, and don't require grain or fancy feed like horses. You've heard they can be stubborn, and it's true they have a mind of their own, but I've found them steady and reliable, pretty intelligent too."

Our conversation went on with Joe Gregg explaining about many other aspects of early Trail travel in answer to my many questions. "I know we're following the scouts, and along here I can see the dips in the prairie where the old Trail went, but how do we know which way to go when the Trail is not so obvious?"

"We're using the Global Positioning System. Jeff Trotman, one of the mounted scouts, has a GPS instrument set with the coordinates of the Trail. We won't get lost with him up there. And I think he and a friend rode our route last month, making sure we could get through this way."

One duty that the early-day Trail scouts did not have was that of opening fences for the wagon train to pass between fields. Our scouts carried wire cutters, pliers, and extra fasteners, let down the barbed wire or pulled it aside, and after the last wagon went through, closed and repaired any breaks. I think they enjoyed saluting the wagons as they went through and, after closing the gap, galloping along toward the front of the train again.

Because we'd had such a late start, it was soon time for supper and camp. The wagons were drawn into a huge circle, and the animals unhitched and tethered out. Several fires were built near the chuck wagon and big iron kettles hung on hooks over them. It wasn't long before the smell of chili with beans filled the air. Tubs of cole slaw and potato salad were ladled out to the lines of hungry travelers. Some campers had brought their own mess kits with tin plates and cups, but with the excuse of saving water for washing up, I could see that the use of paper plates was condoned.

After supper the boys began unloading the wood wagon and soon had a large campfire going. Eddie had found a guitar. A mandolin, accordion, and fiddle player appeared, and we sat around the fire circle to listen and sing along. Trail songs were blended with Scout songs.

Each campfire lights anew
The flame of friendship true
The joy we have in knowing you
Will last our whole life through
And as the embers die away
We know we'll come another day
The Trail will always beckon you
And last your whole life through

Eddie played the guitar and sang his Tecolotito Owlet song, then his favorite, "Piel Canela."

Ojos negros, piel canela
Que me llegan a desesperar
Me importas tu, y tu
Y nadie mas que tu
(Dark eyes, cinnamon skin
Drive me crazy
You matter to me, you, you,
And no one else but you)

He looked soulfully at Helen as he sang, and although she did not have cinnamon skin (piel canela), there was no doubt the song was for her.

The hour grew late, the fire died down, and one of the Boy Scouts bugled Taps from a hill beyond the camp. The group dispersed to find their bags and sleeping spots. A few of the Scouts had set up their little pup tents, but most planned to sleep under the stars. And what stars!

I had never seen them so bright. With the air so clear, and the absence of even the firelight, they sprang out in the velvet sky and seemed close enough to touch. Bright Venus hung low in the west, the Big Dipper floated near the north horizon, and the Teapot constellation dipped toward the southwest with the Milky Way rising like steam from its spout and stretching all across the sky. The breeze died down. A wagon master shouted to the kids to stop their giggling, and finally the only sounds were the shifting and munching of the horses nearby and the occasional steps of the night watch walking by, making their rounds to check on the animals.

Jones, lying near me in her bag, whispered, "Where's Helen?"

"Here, on the other side of me, near the wagon wheel."

"Don't wake her, but I've finally found out where Roylott is. He's with the people who have the big stage-coach. We'll tell her to stay away from it."

I fell asleep more quickly than I believed possible and was wakened only once by the bright moon which rose late in the night. It was past full, declining into a lopsided shape, but still bright enough to illumine the sleeping camp with silver and shadows.

XXIII

Runaway!

Morning came too early, and the leaders, eager to make up for yesterday's late start, fixed coffee only, and the hungry young people had to be satisfied with cold cereal before the animals were hitched up and final preparations were being made. Jones and I walked around the camp looking for Eddie and Helen to warn them about the stagecoach people. But the call to head out came before we could find them, so I climbed aboard the wagon again while Jones walked back along the caravan to continue to search.

Our first difficulty was a stream crossing. There were only a few inches of water, but the steep banks into and out of the stream bed made it a slow and suspenseful crossing. One of the mules toward the end of the procession refused to continue when in midstream, and it took several of the drivers pulling and coaxing to get him to move. The golf cart wagon with its low slung chassis made a wide turn at the approach, hit another rock and overturned, but several hands rushed to help and set it right again quickly. "There's only one more creek to cross," Gregg explained. "No matter how late in the day, the early travelers always crossed and camped on the far side of an arroyo or stream, in case of rising water in the night. See those mountains off in the distance? Rain up there can turn these ditches into rushing rivers, even when it's sunny and clear down here."

As we regrouped and started on again after the stream crossing, Jones and I began looking for Helen. We did not find her, but knew she was safe with Eddie. Eddie later told us that they met Roylott and he congratulated her at following his Trail game so well. Then he invited her and Eddie to ride in the stagecoach. Two of the four women inside gave up their seats and offered to walk for the next stretch, and the two young people boarded.

Speculation differs as to what happened next. One story was that one of the horses had shied at a snake in the path. Another account was that the white bulldog barked at a prairie dog, scaring the horse. Whatever the cause, the horse reared and snorted, alarmed the other horses and began running at full speed. The driver atop the stagecoach tried in vain to slow them. The coach began rocking wildly as it bumped over the uneven ground. A shout went up "Runaway!" and other pursuers followed in an attempt to slow the frightened animals.

Eddie said at that point he realized the danger and speculated that Roylott had purposely set the dog at the horses' heels and that the only way to escape serious injury was to jump out. He grabbed Helen's hand and, opening the door, leaped clear of the plunging coach. They fell rolling onto the yucca and cactus, but except for some scratches and bruises, emerged relatively unscathed.

The other two passengers were not so fortunate. Heading into a deep declivity, the stagecoach was completely upset, slamming the two women inside against the wooden interior. Unable to drag the coach any farther, the horses finally stopped, and when the caravan caught up to them, the women were taken out and given first aid. One woman decided she was merely badly shaken up, but the other suffered what was obviously a broken arm.

We were approaching another fence crossing with a county road beyond it. A cell phone was used to call for help. Luckily we were within calling distance of emergency help. The woman was given first aid, a splint put on her arm, and the kids gathered around to stare at her and at the upset wagon. By the time the ambulance arrived and the unfortunate woman driven away in it, the mounted scouts had opened the fence on the other side of the road and began leading the caravan through.

The horses were calmed, the coach set upright, and we were resuming our trek when a red pickup truck came racing down the road putting up a huge cloud of dust. It stopped at our temporary gate and an angry man carrying a gun got out and began shouting at the rear of the caravan. "Stop! What's going on here! This is private property. No trespassing."

Our march was halted. Gregg and the other leaders came back to talk with the angry rancher. The situation was somehat defused when it was understood that his brother, the co-owner of the ranch, had given permission for the crossing without his knowledge. But instead of acceding graciously, the rancher objected to the great number of people and wagons in the company. The dispute was settled when three of the tractor-drawn wagons volunteered to exit the caravan and return to Clayton. A few of the children and their parents were ready to return, but the remainder declared they had been walking anyway and would continue in the procession. The tiny covered wagon and the golf cart were permitted to continue. Jones graciously offered to be among the numbers who exited. I was surprised at that, but then realized she knew that Roylott had already made his attempt at another "accident" to harm Helen, and he would be leaving to set up his next scheme. Jones intended to follow him.

But, for once, her calculations regarding his next step were mistaken. After the exiled group had left and the caravan had continued on, I spied Roylott in the distance on a big horse riding ahead with the scouts!

Eddie was embarrassed, chagrined, and mortified that he had not protected Helen better. I tried to reassure him. "Jones told me to warn you about the stagecoach," I said. "But we couldn't find you in the morning."

"He was so smooth and courteous to us," said Helen. "His manners were like the old days when my mother was alive, and we felt almost like a family. I blame myself, Eddie. I'm the one who knows his treachery. I feel sorry for the lady with the broken arm. We are lucky to escape, and you really did save me by pulling me out of the coach before it tipped over."

"Now you have some scratches to match my black eye from the brawl," Eddie said, touching her face tenderly. "Roylott is gone and we can enjoy the rest of this journey."

But, looking up toward the west, I saw black clouds forming on the horizon. "I'm afraid we may have more than upset buggies to contend with. I don't like the looks of the sky or the feel of this wind."

XXIV

A Stab in the Storm

My fears were justified. First came the wind, growing stronger and stronger. Covers on the wagons were tightened down, bonnets tied, and coats buttoned against the blast, and following it came the rain in torrents. Everyone wanted to stop and huddle in or under the wagons, but the leaders knew we had one more stream to cross before it became impossible. Slowed by the pelting rain and the buffeting wind, we inched along, hardly able to see in front of us. The horses and mules trudged valiantly onward until we reached Rock Creek. It was already a raging torrent. The scouts led us to the best place for crossing, but the water was up to the hubs of the wheels when the first wagons crossed.

Most of us were wading in the water, the men holding the bridles of the animals to lead them across. One wagon, cutting farther to the left, became mired in the mud, and the horses were unable to pull it up the farther bank. What saved it was the one tractor-drawn wagon that had remained on the trek. After bringing his wagon safely across, he unhitched it and chained the mired wagon to his tractor, pulling it to safety.

Because the storm did not abate, there were no cooking fires, and supper was cold rations meted out from the chuck wagon to the shivering lines of travelers. I waited inside the wagon while Helen stood in the food line wearing her yellow horse-design slicker. Poor Eddie had drawn night-watch duty and was astride a horse going the rounds. As many as could climbed into the wagons; the rest were left to crawl beneath them for shelter. At least our sleeping bags were dry, and I crawled into mine under the wagon, wiggling out of my wet clothes and into the dry ones I had stashed inside the bag. Helen found a dry corner near me also, but there were so many others sharing the space under the wagon, I was forced perilously close to the edge where water was dripping from the wagon top onto the ground. Seeing my plight, Helen threw her yellow slicker over me. My bag and I were snugged up and dry, but sleep was impossible with the thunder and the wind continuing, punctuated with flashes of lightning. I worried that the animals would be spooked by the lightning, but the night crew kept them under close watch.

It was then that I suffered a living nightmare. Almost asleep, I seemed conscious of a dark shape nearby. Thinking it was one of the night-watch boys or Eddie, I half rose to look and realized I had slid farther out from under the shelter of the wagon. Then a sudden flash of lightning illumined a dark form standing over me with a knife-like object in a raised hand. I reacted by rolling to the side and tried to yell as I heard the blow descend, missing me by inches and pinning the bottom of my sleeping bag to the ground. When I finally screamed and Joe Gregg and others came with a flashlight, my assailant had disappeared, and there in the spot where I had lain was a steel rod driven into the ground, through my bag. The top of it was curved into a loop.

"A pickett pin," said Gregg. "And driven in with quite some force. Someone wanted you dead." I knew it was Roylott.

And I knew the stab had been intended for Helen. The yellow horse-design poncho had misidentified his target. Then I remembered the half scrawled message left on the table by the mysterious dark figure on the table in the Kansas City pub. Lucille had tried to warn me. The message was intended to say "Beware the pickett." Gregg showed me the corkscrew-like steel post that was used to tether a horse. The line would be tied in the curved loop at the top of the stake and the corkscrew-like shaft held the stake in place. Lucille really was my guardian angel. She had warned me, and with God's help had sent the lightning that showed me the danger just in time.

I was shaking. Helen was likewise unnerved by the incident. We tried to call the police or the sheriff's office, but the connection was unavailable. Gregg helped us up into the wagon and we spent the rest of the night there, sitting in a cramped space behind the wagon seat. He sat between us with his arms around us. The storm raged, then finally rumbled away and subsided.

In the morning, the sun came out bright again in a clear sky but revealed a sopping and demoralized camp. Eddie returned from his night-watch duty tired and bedraggled. He was disheartened the more to hear about the midnight attacker. We revealed the entire situation to Joe Gregg and were interested to hear that he knew of the spidery man. I assured him that the dark form holding the pickett was not he. His size and the force with which he'd driven the stake down identified Roylott beyond question.

This time there was no question of delaying breakfast. Wood was brought from the wood-wagon, tinder from the cardboard food packages, and the fires were soon kindled for cooking and warming the damp campers. Our camp was in a depression with rising hummocks around us. They were soon spotted with wet clothes laid out to dry, and the terrain took on the appearance of a huge patchwork quilt covering the hillsides. Flapjacks, beans, bacon, and fried potatoes, along with steaming coffee, filled our stomachs and revived our spirits as the sun dried our wet clothes. Morale was restored, the horses given their grain, and we were ready for our final day on the Trail.

Joe Gregg was still interested in finding Roylott, but we determined that Roylott must have ridden off in the storm, perhaps thinking he had at least injured Helen. Gregg sent the scouts and the clipboard lady to survey the entire encampment, taking roll and counting our remaining travelers. Roylott was nowhere to be found.

Eddie slept on the pile of sleeping bags as the wagon rolled onward, up and down over more rolling hills, but across no more streams. We nooned it in a little grove which seemed like the only place with trees for the entire prairie. It had been planted by a homesteader many years ago, and the ruins of the house and barn there were a sad reminder of past efforts to carve a living out of an unfriendly landscape. Helen and I stretched out in the shade of one of the old cottonwoods and regained our energy with a siesta, as did several of the other travelers.

The last night was again clear and cool with no unto-ward incidents. The evening campfire featured ghost stories, and although they were entertaining, they paled in comparison to the real horror story I had lived through. By the time we reached the Rock Point Ranch and saw the waiting cars, we were relieved, but embold-ened by our great trek. The children were eager to tell the stories of the mired wagon, the upset stagecoach, and the storm. Like many who have gone through a trying experience, we felt, in looking back, that it was not so bad after all. But I for one, even though proud I'd survived, did not care to repeat the adventure.

Goodbyes were said, promises to "stay in touch" were exchanged, and the children ran toward their parents, eager to tell of the adventure. One little boy greeted his father with, "I want to go again next year, Daddy, and I want you to come along."

Joe Gregg came toward us carrying a burlap bag bundle. He handed it to me and said, "Here's a souvenir of the trip. Maybe we can ride together again someday." I thanked him and said goodbye. As he walked away, I opened the bundle. There was the pickett pin.

Jones was not at the car, but we found a note from her inside, warning us and directing us for the next stage of the game.

Don't go back to Clayton. Take Amtrak from Las Vegas to Lamy. I will meet you there.

The Train to Lamy

We puzzled over why we should not drive the rest of the way to Santa Fe. Highway 56 joined I-25 at Springer, and there it would be a fast trip south on it down the interstate to New Mexico's capital city at the end of the Trail. But knowing that Jones had more information than we did, we realized that all would be revealed to us later. Another hour brought us to Springer, the town where the auto routes of the Cimarron Cutoff and the Mountain Route came together. The actual Trails, according to our guide-book, did not connect till farther south near Watrous and Fort Union.

The Brown Hotel was the old fashioned stopping place for lunch in Springer. The owners, Debbie and Roy Ackerman, welcomed us and, having heard of the expedition, asked us about our adventures. While we ate fried chicken, we told as much of our story as we could, and they in turn, told us of the nearby Trail site we'd missed in our hurry to get here.

About eight miles back on the road we had traveled, and off to the south on a private ranch was the Rock Crossing of the Canadian River. The crossing became well known and was ideal for the early travelers because the river above it was mostly quicksand, and below it, the river entered a deep canyon, impossible for wagons to negotiate. Also, the rocks were flat and smooth here, affording an easy crossing. "There are gravestones there," said Ackerman. "If you had time, the rancher could tell you quite a story about them."

But we did not have time. We drove on south on I-25 toward Las Vegas. On our left was a huge rocky mountain shaped like a big shoe. Our guide book said the travelers saw it as an outline of a wagon pulled by oxen, and it is named Wagon Mound, with a village of the same name at its base.

Eddie saw the sign for Fort Union and we agreed that it would be a stop on our return with Jones. We heard later that the fort is no longer there but the ruins have been stabilized. The visitor center has a museum and bookstore, and the area is now a National Monument.

We arrived at our Las Vegas train station in mid afternoon and found that luck was with us because the westbound Southwest Chief was several hours late. We would still be able to catch a ride on it from there to Lamy, following Jones' instructions.

When we boarded we went to the observation car where two Park Service volunteers were giving a talk about the Trail features along the way. We asked about the tall sharp peak with the flat top we had passed before arriving at Las Vegas and were told that it was Bernal Peak, often called Starvation Peak, from the legend about beleagured settlers trying to survive there while fighting off a band of Indians.

The taller peak with a rounded hump in the ridge of mountains was named Hermit's Peak, site of the camp, and now a shrine to Giovanni Augustini, the priest from Council Grove, whose cave there we would never forget.

Just as the state of New Mexico is often confused with the country of Mexico on its southern border (for easterners ignorant of their geography), so likewise is the town of Las Vegas, New Mexico, confused with Las Vegas, Nevada. This Las Vegas was once the largest settlement in New Mexico. In the Old Town Plaza is another D.A.R. marker to the Santa Fe Trail, but the Plaza is most famed for the row of buildings near the old hotel. On the roof of those buildings General Stephen Watts Kearny stood in 1846, proclaiming that New Mexico was now a part of the United States.

"Why is Teddy Roosevelt mentioned so much in Las Vegas?" asked a passenger.

"Several of his Rough Riders were recruited from here to fight in the Spanish American War," the speaker answered. "For many years Las Vegas was the place they held their reunions."

Not visible from the train was the Pecos National Monument. Formerly an important pueblo village, it was already abandoned when the Santa Fe traders came through it, but our speaker told us the visitor center is one of the finest and that it has extensive information about the Trail. "Another must-see on our way back," said Eddie.

The little town of Lamy is the station stop for passengers going to Santa Fe, fifteen miles farther north. Jones was waiting for us there, and in answer to our inquiries about the train trip, she explained that she had been in touch with police who warned her that there was a sniper who had fired on cars driving through Glorieta Pass on I-25. Could he be the spidery man, hired by Roylott to watch for Helen's car there? We were approaching the end of the Santa Fe Trail, and was Roylott now resorting to use more drastic measures?

XXVI

Skulduggery in Santa Fe

Jones drove us into town by way of Santa Fe Trail Street, close to the actual route of the original Trail. At Museum Hill we stopped to look at the magnificent Santa Fe Trail Monument, which depicts six mules pulling a wagon out of a muddy stream and headed for the Plaza. The entire structure is over sixty-five feet long and includes four human figures in a dramatic situation. The muleteer, riding on the back of the left mule nearest the wagon, is reaching over to grab the lines of the right rear mule who has stumbled and is regaining his footing. A little boy with his dog is waving his hat to welcome the wagon, while a mounted scout is pointing the way to the Plaza. Nearby an Indian woman turns to look at the group. We loved the information boards with their colorful paintings, especially since we had recently visited many of the highlighted sites. We read about the process the sculptor Sonny Rivera had used to create the master-piece. On a post nearby we pushed the button to hear a man reading from a diary telling of the wagons entering the Plaza in 1852. The sounds of the wagons and the animals created a lifelike background.

The end of the Trail! We could hardly believe we were here. The Plaza was the historic center of New Mexico's capital city and the destination of the Trail traders of long ago. There were several plaques, statues, and buildings to be seen including the famous cathedral, but Jones direct-ed us to the one that we wanted most of all to see, the final D.A.R. marker on a corner across from our hotel. We laughed to see that this marker, the final one of the 170 placed along the Trail, had a map that was incorrect. It depicted the northeast corner of the state as a four-corner junction, instead of three, and showed the Cimarron Cutoff missing Colorado completely!

We strolled the portico of the Palace of the Governors, said to be the oldest, continuously occupied, official build-ing in the country. Native Americans were offering jewelry spread out on blankets along the portico. The silver and turquoise were beautiful, and there were even necklaces made of corn, dyed in bright colors.

Our hotel was La Fonda, the Inn at the End of the Trail. It was also formerly a Harvey House owned by the railroad and serving meals to train travelers. It maintained its historic adobe outline and the interior of beamed ceilings and antique paintings. The hotel has sheltered many famous people including Archbishop Lamy, Buffalo Bill, and even John F. Kennedy. The open patio, now the La Plazuela Restaurant, has been roofed but still admits translucent light, and the live trees there give the feeling of an outdoor garden. The window glass walls have been painted with colorful Spanish motifs. "Let's eat here, tonight," said Helen.

We enjoyed our meal in the pleasant dining room. Occasionally a Native American came by selling souvenirs. We talked with a little boy with beautiful dark eyes who almost persuaded us to buy a kachina doll. Then an older Indian woman came around to the tables with turquoise and silver jewelry to sell. She approached our table with an especially intent look. I believe that she had detected the vibes between Helen and Eddie and suspected that he may be in the market for a special piece of jewelry. "Wouldn't you like this friendship ring for the lady?" she asked. Helen tried on the ring and admired the coral and turquoise setting.

"If it fits, it's yours," said Eddie. And he paid the woman more than she had asked. He leaned over and whispered to Helen, declaring, "That means we're more than friends. We're engaged." Helen blushed, and her smile showed acceptance of the ring and its significance.

The Indian woman seemed reluctant to leave our table. But she was not trying to sell more jewelry. She was looking at me with a strange gaze as she asked, "Have you traveled far? May I read your palm? I do not want money. I am getting signals from my spirit guide. There is a message for you, especially."

We laughed, but I agreed to hold out my hand and wait for her to tell me what she saw there. "You are a strong lady who follows adventure and you have a close friend. You also have a spirit guide, but she is not Indian. She is your guardian angel who is following you to protect you. You have been in great danger, but your angel guide protected you."

I know I must have turned pale. The others were laughing politely, and I tried to join in, but I was over-whelmed by what she had said. She walked away before I could thank her or offer her some money. "That message, just like horoscope messages, could apply to anyone," laughed Jones.

Turning to what they considered more serious topics, I told Jones of my horrific encounter near the wagon, but she said very little about her findings after leaving the caravan. Over dessert she finally revealed the key information. "Roylott is here. He checked into this hotel. But the most interesting thing is that he had his room changed so that he is in the room directly above Helen's. I have booked the room next to Helen's, but I propose that Eddie and I sit on guard tonight in Helen's room while Watling and Helen stay in mine.

We agreed to the plan, but Eddie said he would carry his camp knife with blade open while they waited. After dinner we looked around the foyer and browsed in the lobby shop newstand. "Oh look," I said. "Here's a book by one of the hikers we met on the Trail, *Without A Wagon*. The cover says the author is called Trail Boss. I'll buy it and we can read about the Trail sites we missed along the way." Jones purchased a souvenir Mexican cane, Helen bought some postcards, and we strolled around the Plaza before going to our rooms.

Helen and I sat in the room, refusing to go to bed with the suspense of what may happen next door. I began reading *Without A Wagon* and the adventures of the hiking women managed to keep me awake, but Helen, sitting in an easy chair across from me, began to nod and close her eyes.

It was past midnight, and in spite of the Trail stories I began to wonder if merely dreaming about them would serve as well. The bed looked very inviting. Helen had slumped to the side in her chair and was fast asleep.

Suddenly I heard a banging noise, a loud groan that was partly a scream, and heavy footsteps going by in the corridor. I ran to the door and opened it to see two policemen running down the corridor toward the elevator. I stepped quickly to the next-door room and pounded on the door. Jones opened it and faced me with the cane in her hand, her gray curls tousled, but a look of triumph on her face. "I think it's over," she said.

Then I saw Eddie emerging from the elevator. "I think he's dead," he said. I knew he meant Roylott, but I did not understand how it had come about. Helen had followed me into the hall, sleepily asking, "What's going on?" The three of us went down to the lobby in time to see the two policemen accompanying the medics who were carrying a gurney. One medic was holding an I-V bag connected to Roylott, and they were rushing to the ambulance waiting outside.

"In the words of Sir Arthur Conan Doyle," said Jones, "Violence, does, in truth, recoil upon the violent, and the schemer falls into the pit which he digs for another."

We gathered in Helen's designated room to hear the explanation. Eddie looked triumphant and, putting his arm around Helen, sat with her on the edge of the bed to hear Jones explain how it all happened.

"When I learned that Roylott's room was directly above Helen's, I examined the ceiling carefully. There were sprinkler system taps, beautifully designed as decorative floral studs and two smoke detectors. Why two smoke detectors? I wondered. Because one was a fake, a cover for a hole which had been bored through from the floor above. I wondered if Roylott planned to inject a poisonous gas into Helen's room through the hole. Then I remembered that Eddie had said Roylott was interested in snakes. He reminded me that a snake that was warm and surfeited from recent feeding would appear quite torpid. We should inspect the room carefully.

"He was right. Pulling back the coverlet on the bed revealed a pillowcase concealing the lumpy form of what was probably a rattlesnake. Eddie grabbed the pillowcase, twisted the end shut and threw it into the bathtub. The hole was directly above Helen's bed and we expected that Roylott would listen or peer through to determine the success of his plan. Eddie and I waited, with the lights on, for a decent interval of time, but keeping away from the area which he could see if spying through the hole. Then turning out the lights, we put a row of pillows under the coverlet of the bed to resemble a person sleeping there. But first we pushed a chair close to the edge of the bed; one of us could stand on it and reach the hole with the Mexican cane.

"Our suspicions were correct. After about an hour, the beam of a flashlight shone down onto the bed through the ceiling hole. Then we heard a container being opened and saw the head of a snake emerge from the hole. Eddie jumped onto the bed. I was standing on the chair with the Mexican cane. Roylott pulled the snake back. I poked at the hole, and I thought I must have struck the snake or Roylott because I heard him scream. The snake had attacked him. I think it was to the head or throat because Roylott must have been kneeling close to insert the viper into the hole."

"Who called the police?" I asked.

"I had already alerted the police and informed them of my suspicions. They were waiting in the upper vestibule."

"But won't the anti-venom revive him at the hospital?" Helen asked.

"I heard them say, 'No heart beat detectable' as they went by," said Jones. "We'll know as soon as we call the hospital. And our evening is not yet at an end. There will be questions to answer, papers to sign, and decisions to be made yet. Helen, as next of kin, you will be involved in all of this."

It did prove to be a long night for all of us but one of great relief that the perilous pursuit was over, the villain had succumbed to his own evil, and now Helen was freed from her fears. Roylott had held the second snake in reserve, and when his room was checked, a third one was found in a cage there. But his clever plan did not match the cunning preparations of the famous Sheila Jones.

The coroner's report stated that Roylott had died of a heart attack brought on by the encounter with a poisonous snake. *The Santa Fe New Mexican* newspaper, at the request of the hotel manager, stated that a guest had died of a heart attack and made no mention of a rattlesnake.

I am glad to give my report a happy ending. In spite of Jones' dislike of romantic stories, this record of our most difficult case can be classed as a romance, as well as an adventure and a detective thriller, because Helen inherited the Westport mansion, and she and Eddie were married as soon as she submitted her successful thesis on the Santa Fe Trail to the University of Kansas.

The wedding was held in Council Grove, the place they had met. Jones and I were guests of honor. Aunt Lillian was there, and Helen's sister Julia (now released from her vows) was bridesmaid. Eddie's brother Raoul was best man. The reception was held in the Hays House, the longest continuously operating restaurant west of the Mississippi, and the happy couple rode off in a covered wagon to begin their honeymoon.

Now that the case is closed and I am recording this for Jones' memoirs, I can again state that this was the most dangerous, the longest, and the most thrilling of all our adventures. The phone may ring at any time, inviting me to accompany her on a new case. But as I write here in my Albuquerque apartment, I have this strange urge to revisit the Santa Fe Trail. I look up at my fireplace and see the pickett pin in a place of honor on the mantel. It will soon be spring, and I am remembering that Mr. Gregg said he hoped we could take a wagon ride together again some time. I think I will ask him if that offer still stands.

FINIS

Without A Wagon on the Santa Fe Trail

by Inez Ross

The year was 1996. Three semi-retired women, looking for a challenge, decided to hike the Santa Fe Trail, the first trading route in 1821 that had linked the state of Missouri to the city of Santa Fe in what was then a foreign country. What began as a lark grew into a serious quest to walk the entire 800 miles from Santa Fe, to Franklin, Missouri.

This is the true story of their trek as revealed in the log of their six-times-a-year hikes and in the articles written for the local newspaper. The paperback book has over one hundred photos, plus the song the women composed as they hiked up the Trail.

Dr. James Siekmeier, history professor, says, "Because her articles show a first-hand knowledge and love of the Trail, I used excerpts to enliven my university history class presentations. Anyone interested in the American West will benefit from reading this first-class account."

To order this book, send $11.50, which covers cost of mailing, to

Ashley House
614 47th St.
Los Alamos, NM 87544

The Santa Fe Trail Association

The SFTA was founded in 1986 to preserve, protect, and promote the historic Santa Fe Trail that ran from Franklin, MO, to Santa Fe, NM, from 1821 to 1880. The Trail was designated a National Historic Trail by Congress in 1987, and the SFTA works with the National Park Service to interpret historic sites for Trail visitors.

The Association publishes a quarterly newsletter WAGON TRACKS and sponsors a major gathering every year. In the even-numbered years it's a Trail Rendezvous at Larned KS, and in the odd-numbered years it's a Trail Symposium at a special selected site along the Trail.

Join the SFTA by sending your $25 to Ruth Olson Peters at the Santa Fe Trail Center, RR3, Larned, KS 67550. In addition, to maximize your Trail enjoyment, join one or more of the twelve chapters situated along the Trail.

Missouri River Outfitters	St. Joseph MO
Heart of the Flint Hills	Lyndon KS
Cottonwood Crossing	Newton KS
Quivira	Lyons KS
Wet/Dry Routes	Larned KS
Wagon Bed Spring	Ulysses KS
Texas Panhandle	Amarillo TX
Dodge City/Ft Dodge/Cimarron	Dodge City KS

Bents Fort .Rocky Ford CO
Cimarron Cutoff . . . . .Clayton NM
Corazon de los Caminos . . . . .Springer NM
End of the Trail . . . . .Santa Fe NM

For more information check the Internet at http://
www.santafetrail.org.

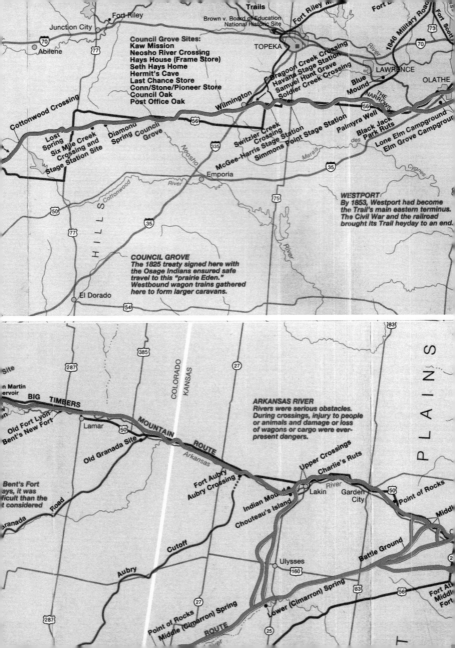

Council Grove Sites:
Kaw Mission
Neosho River Crossing
Hays House (Frame Store)
Seth Hays Home
Hermit's Cave
Last Chance Store
Conn/Stone/Pioneer Store
Council Oak
Post Office Oak

Brown v. Board of Education
National Historic Site

COUNCIL GROVE
The 1825 treaty signed here with
the Osage Indians ensured safe
travel to this "prairie Eden."
Westbound wagon trains gathered
here to form larger caravans.

WESTPORT
By 1853, Westport had become
the Trail's main eastern terminus.
The Civil War and the railroad
brought its Trail heyday to an end.

Dragoon Creek Crossing
Havana Stage Station
Samuel Hunt Grave
Soldier Creek Crossing

Switzler Creek
Crossing
McGee-Harris Stage Station
Simmons Point Stage Station

Palmyra Well
Black Jack
Park Ruts

Lone Elm Campground
Elm Grove Campground

Lost
Spring
Six Mile Creek
Crossing and
Stage Station Site
Diamond
Spring
Council
Grove

Cottonwood Crossing

THE NARROWS

Blue
Mound

Junction City
Fort Riley
Abilene

TOPEKA
Wilmington
LAWRENCE
OLATHE

Emporia
El Dorado

ARKANSAS RIVER
Rivers were serious obstacles.
During crossings, injury to people
or animals and damage or loss
of wagons or cargo were ever-
present dangers.

BIG TIMBERS
Old Fort Lyon
Bent's New Fort
Lamar
Old Granada Site

MOUNTAIN ROUTE

Arkansas

Fort Aubry
Aubry Crossing
Indian Mound
Chouteau's Island

Upper Crossings
Charlie's Ruts

River

Lakin
Garden
City
Point of Rocks
Middle

Bent's Fort
...ays, it was
...ficult than the
...t considered

...aranada Road

Cutoff

Aubry

Point of Rocks
Middle (Cimarron) Spring

ROUTE

Ulysses

Lower (Cimarron) Spring

Battle Ground

Fort At
Middl
Fort

COLORADO
KANSAS

PLAINS